*What kind of love slave would Brittany want?*

Chad could only guess she'd choose the cop or maybe the fisherman, simple guys who didn't turn her on. A guy she could resist and easily ignore. After all, she'd made it plain that she was here under duress. Which meant that she was at the top of Chad's hit list....

"Young man." A sharp voice startled Chad out of his ruminations. He turned to discover Laurel, the irreverent ex-Supreme Court judge rolling her wheelchair up to him.

Shrewdly the octogenarian, unlit cigar clamped between her teeth, cornered him. "You're eavesdropping."

Chad locked gazes with the woman, but spoke calmly, hoping he wouldn't draw further attention to himself. Hoping Laurel wasn't thinking about buying his "services." *More than anything, he hoped she wouldn't pinch his ass again.* "All right, I admit it. I was hiding from you."

"Me? Why?"

"Because I was guarding my flank."

Laurel let the cigar dangle from her thin lips as she grinned wickedly. "With flanks like yours, sailor, you can't be too careful...."

# Blaze™

Dear Reader,

When I first decided to try my hand at writing a book for the new Blaze series, I wanted to tap into the ULTIMATE female fantasy. And what is more erotic than having your very own love slave—a seriously sexy, extremely *talented* navy SEAL, one who is bought and paid for and is dedicated to fulfilling your every desire? And of course, I couldn't leave it there. So I put that gorgeous man and his new mistress in a resort called Eden, with all the decadence the name implies.

Though I've written more than a dozen books for Harlequin Intrigue, I've always focused on romantic suspense. Writing *Enslaved* provided a new challenge—using steamy, sensual encounters to weave romantic and sexual tension. The result is a book I hope will heat up your own midnight fantasies.

Come visit me at www.susankearney.com and check out my upcoming releases, including another Blaze title in the fall.

In the meantime, sit back, relax…and ENJOY!

*Susan Kearney*

P.S. Don't forget to check out the special Blaze Web site at www.tryblaze.com!

# ENSLAVED
## *Susan Kearney*

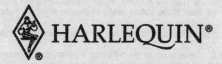

# HARLEQUIN®

TORONTO • NEW YORK • LONDON
AMSTERDAM • PARIS • SYDNEY • HAMBURG
STOCKHOLM • ATHENS • TOKYO • MILAN • MADRID
PRAGUE • WARSAW • BUDAPEST • AUCKLAND

For my editor, Brenda Chin.

Without her guidance, this book would not exist.

ISBN 0-373-79029-5

ENSLAVED

Copyright © 2002 by Susan Hope Kearney.

Visit us at www.eHarlequin.com

Printed in U.S.A.

# 1

"MOTHER, YOU CAN'T buy me a man!"

Brittany Barrington finally let loose the aggravation that had been building for weeks, ever since her mother had decided to stick her famous nose into Brittany's private life.

"But if I *could* buy you a man, would you want him?"

Not in the least perturbed by Brittany's outburst, the woman who'd graced the covers of *Cosmopolitan* and *Vogue* in the sixties perched on the corner of Brittany's desk, her lithe figure a testament to good genes, a healthy diet and the best cosmetic surgery money could buy. But her mother was more than a pretty face and svelte body. The intellect that had built a cosmetics empire in the eighties shone out of Samantha Barrington's green eyes, simmering with well-meaning concern.

Brittany didn't need her mother's concern, her pity or her meddling. What she needed was to be left alone to deal with her private life like the twenty-nine-year-old woman she was. Just because she'd gone through the most embarrassing divorce of the decade didn't mean her mother could come into her office and start rearranging her life. As usual, her mother's interference had Brittany's defensive walls shooting sky-high and her blood pressure rocketing.

Seemingly oblivious to Brittany's annoyance, Samantha walked around her daughter's desk and tapped the computer keyboard. Next year's budget analysis of Brittany's Feed The Hungry Children advertising campaign disappeared from her monitor.

"Hey, I was working," Brittany complained, already knowing it would do no good, since her mother seemed bent on a mission.

"You're always working."

The censure in her mother's voice brought forth an immediate protest. "That's not true. I have a life, Mother."

"A boring one."

Brittany didn't find her life boring. She kept herself busy with her work, her short list of friends, and more work. If she chose to waste her entire life playing solitaire with a deck of fifty-one, it was her business—not her mother's.

Drawing herself to her full five feet eight inches, Brittany kept her voice under tight control. "I'm sorry if my life doesn't live up to your high standards."

"I want you to be happy."

How could she argue with that statement? Brittany would be happier if her mother would leave her alone, but she bit back the sharp retort.

Samantha always meant well. First a gorgeous model and then a powerful executive, her mother was accustomed to getting her way without a smackdown, drag-out fight. Not this time. Although Brittany knew from experience that the harder she argued, the more stubborn her mother would become, she, too, knew how to be resolute.

Fortunately, or unfortunately, she'd inherited that same stubborn trait. Not for the first time she wondered why she couldn't have inherited Samantha's eyes, or her facial structure that practically kissed the photographer's lens and said *I love you,* while it returned the sentiment tenfold. Instead, Brittany's oval face resembled the father she'd never known—the love of her mother's life, a free-spirited hippie who'd died in a motorcycle accident before Brittany had made it out of Samantha's womb.

While Brittany had never received any fatherly advice, she had gotten his wavy blond hair—not near as striking as her mother's chestnut locks—and rather mundane hazel eyes, which while pretty, were nothing extraordinary—and not near as riveting as her mother's deep emerald eyes. Or, for that matter, as vibrant a color as the pair of baby blues that Brittany's ex-husband Devlin had dumped her for.

Not that Brittany blamed her failed marriage on her looks. The charming Devlin hadn't had the ability to remain faithful to any one woman. Brittany's mistake had been that she'd thought she could change him into a man of honor and convictions, naively believing that if she loved him enough he wouldn't stray.

Her mother had brought Brittany up to believe that anything was possible if she believed in herself and if she worked hard enough. Until Brittany's failed marriage, that philosophy had worked. She'd been a straight A student. Popular in the private New York City high school. Accepted at the University of Michigan, the college of her choice where she'd majored in business.

She'd even landed her dream career in New York City, heading up a charity that fed the world's starving children. Brittany had had everything she'd always wanted, until three years ago, when Devlin's philandering had shredded her heart.

According to her mother, she'd been moping and hiding ever since. Brittany preferred to call her withdrawal from most social activities and all dates self-preservation. She was no longer afraid of running into Devlin with his latest girlie-girl on his arm. No, she was simply avoiding another mistake.

Her mother's plum nails waved through the air, slicing through Brittany's thoughts. "Did you check out the e-mail I sent you?"

"Sorry. I haven't had time. I've taken up a new—"

"Hobby? Darling, that's wonderful. I knew you'd enjoy the dance class I arranged for you if you gave it a chance. Are you finding it therapeutic?"

"I don't need therapy."

Her mother's look said that was a matter of opinion. The perfectly shaped brows arching in disagreement allowed Brittany to squash her guilt over the memory of tossing the dance certificate into the trash along with the free massage from Milo. Milo, who happened to be very Italian, very dark, very handsome and very available, was not a man she trusted to run his hands all over her body. And dancing required a dance partner—the last thing she needed was some man leading her around.

She'd been led around enough, thank you very much. "I started a nutrition class at the university."

"That's more work, dear." Samantha called up the e-mail she'd sent Brittany. "You need some fun." She pointed the cursor at an attached file, clicked the mouse and opened it. "How about him?"

The computer screen filled with a picture of a hunk. With black wavy hair, killer blue eyes and a tooth-paste-bright smile, he sported pectoral muscles that suggested he spent more time in the gym than working a real job.

Brittany refused to be drawn into her mother's idea of a fantasy man and let out a sigh of exasperation. "Mother."

Samantha punched another key and called up a blond Adonis in a thong who looked as if he could apply for an audition on *Boywatch*. He had the shoulders of an Olympic swimmer, a lean flat stomach and thighs and a butt that wouldn't pinch an inch.

"He's kind of cute, don't you think?" Her mother watched her, waiting for a reaction.

Brittany refused to give her mother the satisfaction of agreeing. "Maybe you could hire him for your men's cosmetic division."

"Don't you find him attractive?" her mother pressed with a hint of forced sadness.

Brittany ignored her mother's attempt to manipulate her, ignored the green eyes widening with an innocence that almost always elicited a feeling of guilt in Brittany for not going along with Samantha's wishes. Brittany's private life might not be much, but it was hers and she'd like to keep it private. That her mother thought she needed help to find a man was downright embarrassing. Almost as humiliating as the day Samantha had found Brittany crying outside her and Devlin's apartment after she'd walked in on him in their bed with another woman. Brittany had been so stunned, so hurt, she'd pulled into a painful fetal ball. Unable to leave, unable to stay, she'd huddled against the door, trying to understand that her perfect world was no longer the stuff of diary dreams.

Hard work hadn't saved her marriage and neither could her genuine love for Devlin. A one-sided love wasn't enough. The simple fact that it took two loving people to make a marriage work left her paralyzed with a numbing hurt. She'd stayed in a fog that had taken a long time to burn away. She'd learned some hard lessons, the hardest one being that the only person she could completely control was herself.

She exhibited some of that control now, forcing her voice to sound even and calm as she stared at the blond Adonis on the monitor. "I'd have to be blind not to find him attractive, but I don't want to meet him. I certainly don't want you to buy him for me."

"Why not?"

Brittany folded her arms over her chest, sure of her moral ground. "Any man that can be bought isn't worth having."

Her mother shook her perfectly tousled just-got-out-of-bed hair that took hours for her hairdresser to achieve. "Why do you think prostitution is the oldest profession?"

How like her mother to answer a question with another question. Brittany wasn't backing down. "I'm not going to argue with you, Mother. And you're missing my point. *I'm* not interested in a man who's paid to entertain me. The idea's embarrassing."

"You find it embarrassing that a man would work to please you?"

"That's not what I meant and you know it. To pay someone to be one's companion…it's degrading."

"Really? How would you know?" Samantha asked, her voice quiet but steely. "How do you know it wouldn't be glorious? Or fun?"

"Oh, please. Do I have to take drugs to know they're bad for me? Do I have to jump off the Brooklyn Bridge to know it will hurt when I land?" Brittany pressed the delete button and took satisfaction in obliterating the smiling Adonis.

Too bad she couldn't make her mother disappear as easily. She really did have work to finish. She'd skipped lunch and her stomach was rumbling. Besides she didn't need to know that her mother could really buy these men.

Plum nails clicked over her keyboard and erased all the files. "If only your father had lived—"

"Then I wouldn't see everything in black and white," Brittany finished her mother's favorite phrase. "Only this time you're wrong."

"You can't know what you're turning down until you experience a glorious month with a stranger paid to cater to you."

Her mother sounded as if she spoke from experience. Her eyes held a soft glow, her tone, a hint of remembered passion. Brittany didn't want to go there. Just a little over a year ago, her mother had been seriously dating the sculptor Jeffrey Payne, who had dumped her for an eighteen-year-old model. Her mother had been wounded. Brittany knew that, since her mother never spoke the artist's name again. While Brittany didn't know the details of their affair, she knew Jeffrey had moved into her mother's penthouse and they'd shared a bedroom for several months. She didn't want to think about her mother's sexuality. She didn't want to think about her own, either. "I'm not interested."

"You should be interested. How long since you've been with a man?"

"Mother!"

Brittany felt heat rise to her cheeks. Although she should be accustomed to her mother's open attitude toward sex, she could never understand or embrace it. Brittany suspected that the sixties, the Pill, and Make Love, Not War slogans had influenced her mother's perspective. Well, Brittany didn't grow up in the sixties.

Samantha took Brittany's hand, trapping her. "I'd like you to take a vacation with me."

"I don't have time for a vacation."

"Make time. You don't have to participate if you don't want to."

"Participate in what? Therapy?" Brittany asked, but with a sinking feeling in her gut, suspected that she already knew. After her divorce, her mother had asked her if she would be interested in joining a wealthy group of powerful women who vacationed upstate.

"Come to Eden with me."

Eden? The name elicited memories of an unpleasant afternoon, long ago, just after she received her divorce papers, when her mother had tried to coerce Brittany into taking a vacation with her. Samantha had explained enough for Brittany to understand the gist of the secret that was Eden.

Although her mother had never directly said she was a member, Brittany had surmised Samantha Barrington belonged to the exclusive group of rich and powerful women who owned the resort in the Catskill Mountains—a very private club where the members had the clout to keep their activities secret from the prying eyes of the world. On five thousand acres of land, Eden had its own laws, its own police department. And it had one humongous secret.

In Eden, women could buy the services of men.

She wondered if Eden was the reason her mother had never remarried or perhaps Samantha simply dated the wrong men. Brittany selfishly wished her mother would find some man to make her happy because it might mean she'd stop nagging and leave her daughter alone.

Brittany hadn't allowed her mother to take her to Eden after her divorce, and she wasn't going to now. It was too humiliating to think that she was such a failure that she would stoop to buying companionship.

While Samantha almost always got her way, this time Brittany wasn't giving in. No way was she going to Eden.

"THE CODE NAME is Eden."

"Another secret mission, sir?" Lieutenant Chad Hunter prodded his superior officer, who seemed unusually reluctant to get down to business.

But then this entire meeting was unusual. Unscheduled. Unexpected. Secret missions for Chad's Red Squad search-and-rescue-trained navy SEALs weren't usually conducted in a country club bar. And his six-week shore leave hadn't been canceled, which would have occurred if the navy needed him and his specialized team to move out at a moment's notice for trouble in one of the world's hot spots.

Three days ago, he and his men had flown back to Hawaii after the successful rescue mission of a downed pilot off the coast of China. The month before, he'd raced to extract a submarine caught in Arctic ice. Before that, he'd helped United Nations troops escape from the violent coup in Eritrea.

Chad took immense pride in his team's successes, in their ability to be ready to go on very short notice. So far, he'd never lost a man. Never failed in a mission. The navy gave him the tough assignments and, always ready to serve his country, Chad would put his personal plans on hold if necessary.

Packed and heading to Ohio for a well-earned visit to his parents, six sisters and their spouses and the ever-growing assortment of nieces and nephews, Chad had been surprised by the admiral's request to meet over dinner. Yet, he didn't mind a delay. Chad might enjoy some well-earned R and R and a visit with his large family, but he didn't look forward to his sisters' attempts to meddle in his private life.

Chad sipped his beer. Curious, he waited for Admiral Warren Gates to come to the point.

"This isn't an official mission. Would I be interrupting any special plans for your leave, sailor?"

"The usual, sir." Chad helped himself to a pretzel, knowing that eventually the admiral would come to the point of this meeting. The admiral appeared as uncomfortable as a rookie making his first parachute drop from thirty thousand feet, and that made Chad wary. He'd seen Admiral Gates confident on a bridge with sirens wailing while antiaircraft fire hammered his ship, seen him order men to almost certain death, seen him cajole politicians for funding, all without an outward qualm. So when the admiral spoke reluctantly, Chad's sense of danger went on alert, though he kept his tone casual. "I'm planning to see the family, sir."

The admiral's leathery face crinkled in a curious smile. "No special woman?"

Chad frowned at the thought of the matchmaking that awaited him at home. Not that Chad didn't like women. He did. He certainly did. The women he dated were smart, career oriented and as adamant about shying away from permanent attachments as he was. He would see an occasional lady friend on weekend leaves, or sometimes during the week in town when he was free.

Chad grimaced, knowing that back home his sisters were chomping at the bit to fix him up. He'd tried to explain that he would never marry again—not as long as he intended to make the navy his career. He loved his work and enjoyed the excitement of living on the edge, the responsibility of leading men, the satisfaction in saving lives.

He'd learned five years ago that a wife expected her man to come home at night, or at least phone and let her know when she could expect him. His job didn't allow for such civility. Out of contact, he could be gone for hours, days or weeks. It wasn't fair to ask a woman to be satisfied with the times he could be with her. He'd tried to make the marriage work, but Roxy had finally given up and divorced him.

Never again would he leave behind a woman who kissed him with tears in her eyes. One who silently begged him to give up his career to stay home and play house. He couldn't take that kind of guilt trip. It would be fine with him if he never went through that experience again.

"Each of my sisters will have someone picked out for me. Someone with marriage potential written all over her."

The admiral raised a bushy gray brow. "You don't sound too happy over it."

"Sir, I have *six* sisters."

The admiral had actually met two of his siblings when they'd flown in to nurse Chad back to health after he was wounded in Bosnia. Such a fuss over a little shrapnel in his shoulder! During his short convalescence, his sisters had fed him homemade soups, stuffed him with vitamins and drowned him in vegetable tonics until he'd called their husbands and begged them to recall their wives.

The admiral shook his head and chuckled. "If the other four are as determined as the two I met…"

Chad couldn't quite restrain his proud smile. "I assure you they are, sir."

"Then I can understand your reluctance." The admiral paused. "I have an unofficial favor to ask you. A personal favor."

Finally, as Chad had known he would, he'd come to the point of this meeting. "What can I do for you, sir? All you have to do is ask."

Chad would go out of his way to perform any favor this man asked. Not only did he hold the admiral in high regard as a commanding officer, he admired his courage in looking out for his men. The admiral had been willing to knock heads with the brass and pull Chad's butt out of the fire more than once. He and his men very likely owed their lives to this man who'd ordered a chopper extraction to airlift wounded men when they'd been ambushed in a delicate operation off Libya. So not only did he owe the navy admiral for pulling strings and sending in the army Black Hawk, he respected him as a man.

"My son's disappeared."

"Lyle?"

Chad knew Admiral Gates had hoped his son would follow in his own footsteps and make the navy his career. Under Chad's command, Lyle had tried. Chad remembered the man, not just because he was the admiral's son but because he'd been particularly bright. He swam like a frogman. He'd learned the basics of hand-to-hand combat, scuba diving and underwater explosives. A master marksman, he had the courage of ten men, and could plot strategy like a tactician. But as a loner, he'd never fit in, hadn't been happy, and he hadn't re-upped.

Chad had lost track of Lyle. The admiral rarely spoke of him, yet there was no doubt that father and son were still close. Chad could read the concern in the admiral's eyes, could hear the edge in his tone, observe the tense muscles in his neck.

"He signed up for a stint in this place called Eden. And he never came back."

Chad was familiar with most geographical locations that would hire a man with Lyle's unconventional warfare skills and superior intelligence, but he'd never heard of Eden. Yet he and his team were prepared to go into any of the world's oceans, cope with its deserts or tackle its mountains or jungles.

"Is Eden a mercenary camp, sir?"

"No. It's a resort."

"Where?"

"In the Catskill Mountains."

Chad frowned in confusion. "A paramilitary group is operating out of a resort in Upstate New York, sir?"

"Eden's not a military outfit, although I do believe they have a former two-star general. Eden is run by the world's wealthiest and most powerful women. That's about all the recon info I can give you."

Lyle had been captured by a group of women? Recalling the SEAL's expert skills and high IQ, Chad found that hard to fathom. Lyle had specialized in demolitions, but he could pick a lock, fly any aircraft and speak three languages. At a solid six foot four and two hundred and twenty pounds, Lyle had stood eye to eye with Chad. While Lyle was no match for Chad in hand-to-hand combat and the martial arts, he could hold his own against a half a dozen men. The idea of women holding Lyle hostage seemed ludicrous.

But Chad didn't laugh. If he'd learned one thing during his time with the SEALs as leader of his Red Squad of elite men, he'd learned that there were different ways of getting to a man. Blackmail. Kidnapping. Revenge. Money.

Chad pressed the admiral for more information. "I'm afraid I don't understand."

"Specifics are difficult to obtain. The Eden group is select and highly secretive. They have the power, the money and the influence to keep out of the public's eye."

Chad let out a low whistle. For any group to operate in secret within the United States didn't just take a pile of money, it took serious clout and a significant amount of power he wouldn't have thought it possible to muster until this unofficial briefing.

The admiral paused while Chad digested the information, then continued. "We're talking Supreme Court justices, foreign royalty, senators and congresswomen, owners of worldwide corporations, and celebrities, who vacation on over five thousand acres of closely guarded land."

Chad scratched his jaw, finding the entire subject puzzling. "And this group of women have something to do with Lyle's disappearance?"

"He contracted to…go there for a month."

"You think he's still there?"

"I do." The admiral ordered another round of drinks. "I'd like you to infiltrate the Eden operation and bring him back."

"Sir, my team can be ready to insert within five hours."

The admiral shook his head. "You can't go in guns blazing. You have to go in undercover. And alone."

"No backup?"

Chad had complete faith in his team and wouldn't leave them behind without a damn good reason. For any mission to succeed, planning and teamwork were critical. Each of his team members had his own specialty, but could fill in for a wounded teammate if necessary. Success often depended as much upon having the right man in the right place as good preparation. Six heads and six pairs of eyes would do a much better job than Chad could alone. "My men know how to blend—"

"The only men who go to Eden are under contract. Their security is so tight not even a SEAL can sneak in."

"So what's the insertion plan?"

"You insert yourself into their operation the same way Lyle did. A lady has to buy your services."

Chad's gut tightened. He'd performed many unpleasant tasks for his country, but this contract sounded much like…enslavement. "Exactly what kind of services am I selling the ladies?"

"The personal kind."

# 2

"ARE YOU A VIRGIN, young man?"

Surely the eccentric old lady in the wheelchair who was wearing a rhinestone gown and smoking a cigar couldn't be talking to him? But she was.

Chad had entered Eden determined to roll with the punches while he discreetly searched for Lyle. He stood inside a courtyard and gazed down at the blue-haired woman with flinty green eyes and more wrinkles than a shar-pei and wondered if he was mentally prepared to take on the mission that Admiral Gates had arranged.

The ladies sure ran a first-class operation. From the moment he'd received the overnighted contract, Chad's life had been arranged for him. He'd flown to New York and the following day the limo driver had picked him up from a five-star hotel and driven him straight to the Catskill Mountains.

His chauffeur had told him that the first installment of his generous payment had been wired, and if he wished to check on the deposit's arrival in his account, he could use the car phone. Then the driver reminded him he wasn't allowed to make any other calls, another contract condition. There would be no contact with the outside world during his stay at Eden. Any attempt to violate the communications blackout would bring about immediate dismissal.

Less than an hour ago, the chauffeur had driven Chad through Eden's private gate onto a well-paved road through a gently rolling hillside that skirted larger mountains. Sparsely populated, the resort area had been made famous in the movie *Dirty Dancing*. He'd wryly wondered if the film had given Eden's owners the idea for the resort.

One hundred yards around the first bend, alert security guards had requested both the driver's and Chad's retinal scans before allowing them to enter. Polite and efficient, the guards examined the car, the luggage and its occupants as thoroughly as any military team during a state of war.

These women took their privacy very seriously. Eden's surveillance setup was even more comprehensive than what he'd been led to expect. At regular intervals, he spotted state-of-the-art fiber-optic web cameras that could zoom in on every square inch of the two-mile road. The electric fence line posted No Trespassing signs. Paparazzi wouldn't sneak in here. Neither would curious tourists who might wander by, claiming they'd lost their way.

Just as impressive as the technical equipment were the security teams, which would make his mission more difficult. Not only the gates were guarded. Chad also spotted several patrols with alert dogs making perimeter checks.

Obviously the women who ran Eden demanded the

best, and the efficiency of the employees told him a lot about their employers' demands for privacy.

Although Chad had considered smuggling in technical equipment, the admiral had warned against it, and he'd been glad he'd heeded the advice after the guards passed his luggage through an army-class weapons scanner. These women not only could afford the best security teams, but they apparently had access to classified information and specs on military gear.

Several miles farther inside the resort, the driver turned onto a side road that swept past well-tended lawns and around the sloped hillside in a graceful curve between towering firs to the hill's crest. The architect had taken advantage of the site to build a replica of a medieval castle with all the amenities— including more fiber-optic security and web cams discreetly focused on both the main and side entrances.

Further ahead, he could see the silhouette of a small city that, he recalled from a map was the entertainment district with restaurants, theaters and private rooms designed for a night of pleasure. Tonight, the party was larger and located in the grandeur of a movielike setting.

The chauffeur stopped under a big porte cochere, which reminded Chad of a long-ago era when ladies and gentlemen arrived at balls in shiny black carriages pulled by teams of well-matched horses. Stretching out to either side of the arched entranceway were identical wings.

His driver pointed past a fountain. "The party's that way, sir."

Adhering to the unnecessary directions, Chad followed several couples into a vast courtyard that was paved with black marble and decorated with statues of the Greek gods and goddesses—Zeus, sweeping a wanton shepherdess into his powerful arms, Poseidon, rising out of the sea to kiss an enthralled mermaid, and Aphrodite, tall, strong, erudite, smiling down on the crowd in approval.

Chad straightened the collar of his thousand-dollar jacket, courtesy of Eden, shook out the creases in his slacks and walked into the crowd, paying close attention to the men, searching for Lyle. He noted right off that not only the men but the women wore elegant gold name tags, some of them encrusted with jewels.

To blend in, Chad had helped himself to a lobster canapé and a flute of champagne, wandering past groups of people and scoping out the premises, doing nothing to hide his interest in his surroundings. Anyone new would take in the elegant ambience, sightsee a little, maybe ask one of the ladies for the grand tour.

While he took advantage of being alone, he knew he couldn't go unnoticed. Overhead video cameras captured every angle of the courtyard and his every move.

Women of various ages and nationalities chatted with their male counterparts with a surprisingly sophisticated ease. Although the ratio of men to women was in the ladies' favor, they regarded the men with varying degrees of interest and…respect?

As he observed the well-dressed and well-groomed women, he recognized several. A famous comedienne. A senator. A television commentator. The two-star general the admiral had warned him about.

Then he'd bumped into the cigar-smoking woman in the wheelchair, who seemed intent on waylaying him. With the live music, violins and a flute playing among the chatting crowd, maybe he had misheard her. The old woman's impertinent question definitely seemed out of place in the assembly of elegant men and women dressed in tuxedos and gowns who chatted politely as they ate delicious-smelling delicacies and sipped from crystal flutes of champagne. A mixer, his contract called it.

Even after the long plane ride, his ears should have cleared by now. Still, maybe Chad had misheard. "Excuse me, ma'am?"

She let the cigar dangle from her thin lips. "I asked if you were a virgin. Seems a simple enough question."

From the twinkle in her eyes, Chad could tell the old woman was enjoying his discomfort. "Ma'am, I don't believe that's any of your business."

"Oh, fiddlesticks." She blew a smoke ring at him. "Everything inside Eden is my business. I'm one of the founders, you know."

"I didn't know." Chad bit back a groan. Great. He hadn't been here two minutes, and he'd already offended someone important. He only hoped her eyes weren't sharp enough to read his name tag so she could have security find him and throw him out.

"However, young man, I believe you jumped to conclusions. I was asking if this was your first...*visit.*"

"Yes, ma'am. I guess it shows," Chad confided, feeling foolish and edgy, but confident he could smooth over his mistake with some of the charm his sisters wanted him to use to find another wife. Accustomed to dodging bullets, he required more than a faux pas to make him sweat. "I don't know a soul. I'm not really sure whether coming was a good idea."

She scowled at him, her eyes losing their amusement and taking on a shrewdness that told him she hadn't yet lost all her marbles. "Didn't you read the contract you signed?"

What had he done wrong, now? Chad's signed contract, a thirty-four-page document, had required an attorney to explain the fine points.

"I understand my services have been purchased by Eden Incorporated for one month."

"That's correct. Either you will remain in the dating pool, or your services can be purchased at a premium by one woman for a specified time period. Of course, you'll earn a larger bonus if someone chooses to hire you on an exclusive basis. That could happen. You're a red-hot number if I ever saw one." She gave him a thumbs-up.

Chad didn't know if being a red-hot number was a good thing in his situation, and he didn't know which option he preferred. Staying in the pool might give him access to a wider variety of people during the nightly functions, yet his daytime freedoms would be curtailed and limited to the one luxurious area set aside for men only. On the other hand, if a woman purchased his exclusive services, he'd have more latitude to move around day and night, making it easier to search for Lyle and plan a rescue.

The woman winked at him through her cigar smoke. "The tips can be quite hefty if your services turn out to be in demand like the last SEAL that came through here. The contract guarantees it."

Chad didn't so much as flicker one dark eyelash over her mentioning another SEAL, but her comment was the opening he needed to talk about Lyle. He had no doubts the man would have been popular with the ladies and wondered if the ex-SEAL's contract had been purchased by one woman or if he'd remained in the pool. Careful not to let his curiosity show, Chad shrugged. "Maybe I'll look him up, and he'll offer me tactical advice."

"I'll give you tactical advice. You want to be in demand? All you have to do is look a lady in the eyes and smile."

The woman wasn't going to cooperate, and he wouldn't overplay his hand. He dropped his questions about Lyle for now, a little concerned about the way she was encouraging him to flirt with her. Being in demand was the last thing Chad wanted, especially with a female old enough to be his grandmother. On impulse, he gave her his most disinterested expression.

He still couldn't be sure what kind of personal services his contract required of him. He felt as if he'd been dropped into hostile territory, behind enemy lines, surrounded by land mines with no map—and he had no intention of sleeping with the enemy. However, to fulfill his mission, he had to be adaptable. Even he didn't know how far he was willing to go. Saying no to the wrong woman at the wrong time could end his mission before it began. And while he wasn't prepared to fail, neither was he prepared to surrender.

"You seem very familiar with the contract, ma'am." He tried to make his voice soothing and placating.

"I should be familiar with it since I wrote the damn document," she snapped.

For the first time, Chad looked at her name tag. *Laurel.* Recognition rocked him back on his heels as he mentally filled in the missing last name. She was Laurel Carson, the second woman to have retired as a U.S. Supreme Court justice. Again he'd stuck his foot in his mouth. For a moment he wished he had a trap door beneath his feet for a quick escape. Laurel Carson had the reputation of being one of the sharpest women in Washington, and he'd insulted her, not once, but twice.

Chad reminded himself that SEALs did not run from little old ladies in wheelchairs—no matter how quick their wit. Whatever she threw at him had to be easier than SEAL training.

"Ms. Carson—"

"Laurel. We go by first names in Eden."

He fell back on SEAL training now, knowing a

good offense often beat a good defense. "Ma'am, the contract's specific and generous on monetary matters, but a little vague elsewhere."

"Young man, all you need to remember is that after you leave here, you may not speak about Eden without violating your contract. You can't sign a movie or book deal or go on a television talk show. You can't reveal the name of anyone you meet in Eden or what we do here without risking immediate and severe legal action."

"Yes, ma'am."

By telling the admiral about Eden, Lyle had broken his contract and Eden's rules. Had someone discovered that he'd talked? If so, how far would Eden's founders go to protect their secret? Chad wondered if Lyle could have suffered dire consequences for breaking Eden's code of silence. Laurel Carson would certainly know, just as she knew he and Lyle were both SEALs. Was she warning Chad off?

While the ladies used financial inducements to bribe the men to keep quiet, when that didn't work, they threatened legal action. Had Lyle broken more rules than simply talking to the admiral? Was that why he'd disappeared? Or was he still being held captive somewhere on Eden's premises? Chad refused to consider the third possibility, that Lyle could be dead.

Laurel rolled her eyes at the sky and then puffed on her cigar as if she'd run out of patience with Chad. "If you find this place so disagreeable, your contract gives you the option to leave and never return."

Which all sounded very legit, very unslavelike—

except that six months ago Lyle Gates had signed the same contract Chad had, and that SEAL had never come home.

There was no point in worrying about dangers Chad had no control over. SEAL training had done a thorough job of teaching Chad to compartmentalize. When he jumped out of an airplane or swam out of a submarine into hostile territory, he concentrated only on what he needed to keep him and his men alive. Extraneous concerns weren't forgotten, but prioritized. Right now his main worry was assessing the situation, scoping out the territory and remaining undercover while employing damage control.

Chad did some fast backpedaling and replaced his frown with a warm smile. "I'm upset with myself for not recognizing you right off. You look much younger in person."

Laurel Carson shook her blue-white curls as if she saw right through his tactics. Then she took a crisp white handkerchief from her purse and deliberately dropped it on the marble floor, then peered at him expectantly.

Unfortunately the woman's crazy antics had attracted the attention of several men and women. Chad had lost his opportunity to stay out of the spotlight. In fact, he'd become the center of attention among the small group.

A quick perusal revealed several in the group were amused, several irritated. One woman, a long-legged blonde with wavy hair and guarded hazel eyes, looked as uncomfortable as he felt. When her wary gaze accidentally brushed his, Chad sensed a skittish anxiety that immediately piqued his interest. Except for her eyes, she managed to look calm and contained, although there was no missing the impression she'd rather be anywhere but there. An interesting paradox.

When she noticed him sizing her up, she flicked her serious stare at him in a bold countermove—but divulged a weakness by being unwilling to let her gaze settle too long.

The blonde turned away, her tag flashing the name Brittany, which stamped in his mind as Laurel cleared her throat and drew his attention.

Chad decided his best move was to play Laurel's silly game. That's when the old lady took him by surprise and outmaneuvered him. He bent to retrieve her hanky, and she pinched his ass.

"Laurel!"

The sting of her sharp nails penetrated first his flesh, then his brain, and Chad did what any red-blooded American male would do when facing a flirtatious, cigar-smoking, eighty-year-old woman in a wheelchair. He tossed the hanky in her lap and retreated a step.

Laurel waved her cigar with amusement. "I was only testing the merchandise. And very fine merchandise, it is."

One of the men approached her. "Ma'am, if I was wearing my uniform, I could arrest you for sexual harassment."

"Fiddlesticks." She pointed her cigar at the cop.

"You're on vacation, sonny. Don't get your shorts in a twist."

Chad let the conversation swirl around him while he took his bearings and regrouped. A woman stepped between him and Laurel. Recognizing her was a no-brainer. The Face of the Sixties needed no name tag. Samantha Barrington had been a cover girl, then opened her own multi-million-dollar cosmetic firm. He calculated swiftly and realized Samantha had to be at least in her fifties, but easily looked a decade younger.

While Samantha gently asked the ex Supreme Court justice if she'd remembered to take her medicine today, his gaze slid past a soap-opera actress to the cool Brittany. The fancy name suited her, with her blond hair pulled into a tight twist at the back of her head, her full lips and finely arched brows. Those brows were drawn into a frown on her heart-shaped face, making her appear weary of the entire mixer, as if she had things to do elsewhere and would rather be there than here. When his gaze caught hers this time, she looked right through him.

That's when he noticed Brittany's dress. Red-hot. Tight. What intrigued him was how she'd tried to hide the sexy number with a navy blazer that might as well have been body armor. He found her red dress a direct contrast to her disinterested attitude. A formfitting gown that knotted beneath saucy breasts, a hip-hugging skirt slit to the thigh and spiked ruby heels. Silver hoops dangling from elegant ears. The combination had his senses firing on full automatic.

"Are you okay?" Samantha turned her attention back to Chad as Laurel rolled away.

"I'm fine. I appreciate the rescue." Chad offered his hand and Samantha leaned forward and kissed him on the cheek.

As she bent near him, she took the opportunity to whisper in his ear, "Laurel's a little out there."

"I understand." There was nothing intimate about Samantha's kiss and the sexuality she wore like expensive perfume did nothing to turn him on.

It was Brittany who gained his attention like a heat-seeking missile to a hot target. Her arsenal—the proud tilt of her graceful neck, the angled arrogance of her delicate jaw and the squared ready-to-do-battle shoulders—practically shouted her disdain for the entire mixer. So why was she here? Had she been to Eden so often she'd become world-weary?

Again Samantha drew his attention. "Why don't you introduce yourself to all of us and explain why you agreed to come here?"

*To infiltrate and kidnap a man.* "I'm a navy SEAL on shore leave. I could tell you the extra money sounded attractive, but that wouldn't be completely accurate." Chad had had enough uncomfortable conversations with his sisters to realize that Samantha wanted to analyze his feelings. He figured he'd better give her what she wanted before he antagonized another woman. Keep it simple. Stick to as much of the truth as possible. He tried for his best sheepish grin. "I like new experiences, and I've never let a woman buy my services before."

"Exactly what services would you be selling?" asked a woman at the edge of the group whose name tag he couldn't read.

Great. Of course she would have to ask about the one critical item that the contract hadn't specified. Chad glanced at Brittany, who'd just yawned, and he decided she needed a wake up call. "I'd be selling whatever the lady wanted to buy. It's been my experience that each woman is different."

"Could you give us some examples?" asked Marianne, a redhead with a thousand-watt smile and come-hither eyes.

"Sure," Chad replied easily as he looked straight at Brittany, hoping by nailing her personality publicly, he'd crack the glacial ice in which she'd wrapped herself. He'd decided she would be perfect. Unlike the other ladies, she clearly didn't want to be here. In his eyes, that made her a super-attractive candidate to purchase his services. She wouldn't expect much—certainly she wouldn't want more than he was willing to give. "Some women like to pretend they aren't interested, but they simply need a little coaxing."

Bingo! His words had the desired effect. Brittany's cheeks flushed, but she never lost her cool composure.

Chad continued, his voice soft, deliberately husky. "Some women are icy on the outside but need the right man to heat them up." He let his gaze drift back to Marianne. "Others are ready to have fun almost right away."

"What's your definition of fun?" Gloria asked. Immaculately groomed and attractive, she had eyes as hard and dark as obsidian. Chad prayed she disliked him on sight as intensely as he did her.

"Fun means everyone is enjoying themselves. I have many interests." Chad thought of his sisters and their different hobbies. Chelsea liked to barrel-race her quarter horse. Tiffany was into extreme skiing. Beth crocheted baby blankets. When they tried to fix him up with dates after his divorce, each of them had told him what had attracted them to their husbands.

Their answers had been as varied as their interests. The one thing his sisters all agreed upon was that women found a man's undivided attention to them sexy. Armed with this inside information, Chad had always felt he'd had an edge. He knew how to treat a woman, knew how to make her feel good. "I try to find activities we *both* enjoy."

"Can you describe a perfect evening with a special lady?" came a request from next to Brittany, making it easy to focus on her.

He restrained a grin of satisfaction as Brittany almost squirmed out of her heels. He definitely had captured her attention. Now all he had to do was convince her that he was the one she wanted. "The date would depend on the lady. I like to take my time and savor whatever I'm lucky enough to be offered. A glass of wine. A candlelit meal where we sample good food, talk over soft jazz and share mind-blowing kisses."

"Mind-blowing kisses?" Brittany blurted in a tone

both sophisticated and sexy. She seemed surprised that she'd spoken aloud.

Gotcha!

"My specialty." He didn't bother to contain a lilt of triumph in his tone. "Which wouldn't be special if I handed them out to everyone."

Brittany's eyes widened with curiosity, but her tone held a tinge of challenge. "Does that mean you object to being shared?"

She wanted to share him with another woman? He swallowed hard, then almost choked as he wondered if she could possibly be thinking of sharing him with another man! He knew nothing about these women. He knew nothing about Ms. Disinterested Brittany, whom he might have read wrong. Maybe she was a swinger—a jaded paramour who'd consider his sex play as tame as a house cat's.

As he hesitated, her mouth twisted up in amusement, and he realized she was baiting him, enjoying herself as she put him on the spot. He supposed he deserved it after the way he'd stared at her during the entire conversation, especially after she'd made it so obvious that she wanted to be elsewhere. By the force of his personality, he hadn't allowed her to hide. Now she was defending herself by attacking him. At least there was spunk behind the blasé attitude she'd attempted to portray.

He needed a snappy answer but didn't have one, so he fell back on the truth. "I take pride in leaving my dates satisfied, so a third party would be unnecessary."

Several women murmured to their friends. A few actually nodded in agreement, but Chad kept his eyes on Brittany, who held his stare with a reckless show of courage. She'd challenged him, and she wasn't about to back down, yet her face was bright with color, almost as if she was embarrassed by the entire conversation.

When Samantha leaned over and whispered in Brittany's ear, Brittany shook her head, said something back and lowered her eyes. Chad would have given the month's salary to have heard what they'd said, especially after the group drifted away for other conversations and fresh drinks. Brittany ignored him, not even glancing in his direction. Samantha looked over her shoulder at him with the oddest expression in her eyes—one that he feared was genuine interest.

Chad could only take satisfaction in the knowledge that he'd pricked Brittany's balloon of solitary detachment. Tomorrow night, he would share a barbecue dinner with the women, and he would arrange to sit next to Brittany.

"YOU LIKED HIM, didn't you?" Samantha asked Brittany as they drove a golf cart from the main house back to the luxurious mountain retreat Samantha had built on the lakefront.

"Who?" Brittany had given in and let her mother bribe her into coming to Eden. She'd let Samantha talk her into wearing clingy babe attire, but she wouldn't give her mother the satisfaction of knowing that Chad Hunter had piqued her interest. She'd been unable to resist her mother's promise to finally give her complete control over her trust fund six years early if she stayed in Eden for a month, and she'd intended to remain completely aloof from the men who came here. She planned to pick a different man from the available pool each night, becoming close to none of them.

She'd fully meant to find a man for her mother, figuring if Samantha was busy, she wouldn't have time to interfere in Brittany's life. Instead of thinking about and evaluating suitable candidates for Samantha, Brittany's thoughts kept returning to Chad.

Why had he kept staring at her? She wished she could blame the provocative clothing her mother insisted she wear to put her in the mood, but Brittany suspected that Chad was one of those rare men who looked below the surface. With no words exchanged between them, he'd pegged her personality. Somehow he'd known she hadn't wanted to be there, and he'd used it to his advantage, taunting her with his words, teasing her with that husky voice.

Her mother drove the golf cart and waved as she passed another cart. "The navy SEAL. The one with shoulders as big as my mountain and eyes as dreamy blue as Aquamarine Lake."

"If you like Chad so much, buy him for yourself," Brittany muttered. She didn't care how private or luxurious the resort, she didn't believe in purchasing a man's services.

Her mother arched a perfectly shaped eyebrow. "You remember his name?"

Of course she remembered his name. How could she forget him when she'd found Chad's answers so disturbing? His mere presence in Eden troubled her. How could such a highly trained man, who risked his life for his country, be willing to demean himself by selling his services to the highest bidder? That he was here should have disgusted her enough to lose all interest in him.

But it hadn't. His easy confidence had intrigued her. His charm, which reminded her too much of Devlin's, made her wary. She suspected Chad could have handled whatever questions the group had lobbed at him simply because he was comfortable in his own skin. His self-confidence attracted her, and it left her too aware of her own inadequacies.

Samantha made a sharp right and headed through the security gates into her private driveway. "If I were twenty years younger, I'd outbid you for him."

Was her mother sensitive about her age? Unlike many retired models, Samantha had a fantastic career, but Jeffrey Payne may have done some damage since he'd left Samantha for a woman less than half her years.

"Mother, you look young enough to be my sister. If you don't tell him your age, he'll never know."

"I would know. As much as I admire a youthful physique, I prefer a man of my own generation."

How did her mother always know what she wanted? Brittany knew that her mother wasn't simply putting on an act. Samantha had told her the trick to success was twofold. The first part was the hardest.

She had to figure out what she wanted. Part two was easier, that was simply going after it.

Unfortunately, Brittany never seemed to get past part one—at least not since her split with Devlin. And hanging around her self-assured mother made her feel worse. At least Samantha was leaving by the end of the week. Once she assured herself that Brittany would go through with their bargain and spend the entire month in Eden, Samantha would pursue her own interests. Brittany had flat out told her she had no intention of making love with a stranger and Samantha had agreed with a shake of her head, saying she was willing to let nature take its course. In return, Brittany had promised to spend eight to ten hours a day with a man, attending the activities the resort provided.

Although she'd scouted several interesting men to match up with her mother, she flushed with humiliation just thinking about choosing men from the pool for herself. It wasn't like going to the grocery store and squeezing melons to decide which was ripest. The decision was personal. That Samantha had found it necessary to accompany her only proved to Brittany that her mother didn't trust her daughter's judgment any more than Brittany did.

"So if Chad didn't impress you, what about the lawyer? He was cute."

"If you like pretty boys."

Every man they'd talked to today had been physically appealing, the variety of men and their occupations astonishing. "The policeman had a nice body and a surprisingly good haircut."

The cop's tight pants had been extremely revealing. "Your neighbor Babette wanted him so badly she was fanning herself."

"Babette isn't interested in what's between a man's ears," her mother acknowledged.

Brittany hated to admit to herself that the only man there today who had made her pulse leap and her mind thrum was Chad. He'd worked the group of ladies surrounding him like a master, displaying an almost irresistible combination of warm masculinity and cool charm. Brittany found his boyish allure all the more fascinating since it came from a man with a keen mind and a powerful body.

Chad would fit in anywhere, at a charity ball or in the ghetto. Those large hands of his would be just as at home doling out soup to the hungry as expertly fondling a woman. And that was exactly the reason she didn't want him.

Someday she planned to get involved again—but not yet. She was still too vulnerable. Besides, she definitely didn't want the type of man she'd find in a place like Eden.

She wasn't ready for a man who made her stomach flutter, who made her feel feminine—even for an instant. She most certainly didn't want a man who challenged her.

Tomorrow, she'd let her mother choose someone to partner her at the barbecue, anyone but Chad Hunter.

# 3

AT THE BARBECUE, Chad planned to make his move and tag his prey.

After twenty-four hours spent in the luxurious men's quarters, he'd finished a thorough reconnaissance of the area. While shooting hoops, swimming laps in the heated fifty-meter pool and dining on gourmet food in the sumptuous banquet hall, he secretly analyzed security and timed the perimeter checks. He could beat the tight security, but he figured the risk of getting caught was unacceptable if he could finagle a better angle.

Brittany still looked like his best ticket. Her total lack of interest in the men made her a perfect target. Instinct told him she wouldn't want intimacy from any man, including himself. He simply had to make sure she'd appreciate his companionship.

Aware that asking too many questions about Lyle might cast suspicion on himself, he'd kept his ears open, his mouth shut about his real mission, and introduced himself to as many of the men as possible, casually mentioning that he was a SEAL on leave. He'd hoped someone might again mention Lyle, but no one had, a fact not too surprising since the turnover proved to be high. The women liked to bring in new groups of men every few months.

An hour after his swim, Chad entered the entertainment area, a large open space, well designed to promote conversation and mingling. It was some barbecue. Chad had expected an outdoor event with plastic plates and throwaway utensils. Tables with lacy linen cloths and aromatic floral pieces beckoned diners to use the open seating. Upbeat music filtered through the sound system at a decibel that made conversation easy.

The high-ceilinged room created a relaxed atmosphere with a great selection of pool tables, pinball machines and the latest in 3-D gaming technology. A sumptuous buffet with china, crystal goblets and gleaming silverware was spread along one wall where he spied Brittany in line beside Aurora, a ten-thousand-dollar-a-day model.

Aurora, at six foot two, would draw the gaze of every man in the room. She might be perfect in front of a camera, but to him she looked anorexic. His gaze focused on Brittany's more appealingly wholesome body. She appeared happy to stand in the famous model's shadow. After the way Chad had singled Brittany out during their conversation yesterday, he suspected she didn't want him to join her and would prefer the model's company.

Simply dressed for the barbecue, Brittany wore jeans, a silk blouse and her silver hoop earrings. She'd pulled her wavy blond hair back in a slick-looking ponytail and secured it with a barrette that his fingers itched to remove.

Aurora nodded as Brittany said something and Chad advanced, taking advantage of the cover of potted plants to avoid detection. When he finally tagged Brittany, he didn't want her surrounded by friends—but alone.

"Met anyone interesting?" Brittany asked Aurora.

The model handed Brittany a napkin and nodded toward a man at the salad bowl. "Ryan's file says he's a pianist. A light touch like that might be what I need."

Brittany didn't respond, shifting from foot to foot as if uncomfortable with the frank talk. She might not be pleased, but Chad had picked up valuable information. Until now, he hadn't realized the women had files about the men, which meant it was likely that somewhere in Eden, if he could find it, was data on Lyle. He put the information on the back burner, concentrating on keeping pace with the women as they filled their plates with baby-back ribs, sweet-smelling chicken and medium-rare beef.

On Brittany's other side, Samantha, dressed in snug capri pants and a skimpy top more appropriate for someone younger, leaned forward and spoke to Aurora. "Ryan's a second-timer. I believe Gayle was very satisfied with him. You can look up his rating on..."

Chad peered through palm fronds and watched Brittany's hazel eyes turn stormy. "Please don't tell me you all rate the men's performance in bed."

"Only in my dreams," Aurora chuckled.

Samantha waved a manicured hand at a woman going the other way while keeping up her end of the conversation. "Nothing so crass. We rate the men by how well we like them."

"There's a difference?" Brittany said disdainfully, which made her unique, since the other women around her obviously felt differently. Even Aurora, one of the most beautiful women in the world, seemed perfectly content with the concept of hiring a man.

As the women moved along the buffet line, Chad trailed them. When they reached the desserts, they'd come to a narrower part of the room. The far end, which was darkened, held a dance floor lit only by lanterns that shone on several couples as they gyrated to a soft beat.

Aurora leaned forward slightly, her appreciative gaze following one man's movements. A lady Chad couldn't see spoke loudly enough for her voice to carry. "He can flip my skirt anytime."

Aurora grinned. "I think I'll make Francois an offer he can't refuse."

"I suppose there's no accounting for taste," Brittany murmured, then bit her lip as if to try and stop herself from saying more. Eventually, after a pause, her lips parted on a long, silent sigh. "Aurora, would you mind me asking why you chose him?"

"He's eye candy," the model responded without hesitation.

"They're all eye candy," Brittany protested as Samantha elbowed her to keep quiet.

Comments from other ladies in the buffet line came fast and furious. "Imagine all those muscles on top of you."

"Under you."

"Inside of you."

"Francois is a rock-hard slab of honey-coated beef."

"He sure knows how to move," Aurora murmured.

Undeterred by Samantha's elbow in her side, Brittany shot the model a perplexed look. "He's what you want?"

Between the leaves of the potted palms, Chad watched Aurora shake her head. "That's not all I want. From his file, I get the distinct impression he's shallow."

Irritation and confusion warred in Brittany's hazel eyes. "You have a thing for shallow men?"

"Absolutely. I'm not looking for love. Just lust. And with those fab moves of his hips, he has all the angles I'm looking for."

"But—"

"You want to know why, with my looks, I'm here, why I need to buy a man?"

"The thought crossed my mind," Brittany admitted, her tone tart as she ignored Samantha's scowl.

Chad's curiosity matched Brittany's. He wondered if the women were old friends or new acquaintances, since they sure had different values. And why did Samantha feel as if she had the right to censure Brittany's comments?

Aurora didn't seem to mind speaking candidly.

"The men I know are either gay, or they want something I don't want to give them."

"Yet you're more than willing to give that something to Francois," Brittany pointed out.

Aurora shook her head. "You don't understand. I want a relationship, but the men I meet see my face and my body and my money. They never see *me*. With Francois, I pay up front and we both know what we're getting. Afterward, we both walk away happy. No sticky attachments. No hurt feelings. No messy publicity. No expensive lawsuits."

And what did Brittany want? Chad could guess she'd choose the cop or maybe the fisherman, simple guys who didn't turn her on. A guy she could resist. A guy she could easily ignore. All of which put her at the top of Chad's hit list.

"Young man," a sharp voice startled Chad out of his ruminations.

He turned to discover Laurel rolling her wheelchair right up to him. With the plants at his back, he had nowhere to run.

Shrewdly the octogenarian, unlit cigar clamped between her teeth, cornered him. "You're eavesdropping."

"I am not."

"Are too."

Chad locked gazes with the former Supreme Court justice, but spoke mildly, hoping they wouldn't draw further attention. Hoping she wouldn't pinch his ass again. "I was simply admiring the potted palms."

"Like hell you were. Young man, I demand to know what you're really up to."

He searched for an opening between the pots with his foot as he spoke. "All right, I admit it. I was hiding from you."

"Me? Why?"

"Because I'm guarding my flank."

She let the unlit cigar dangle from her thin lips as she grinned wickedly. "With flanks like yours, you can't be too careful."

He saw the gleam in her eye and the tremor in her reaching hand. Before she could pinch him again, he backed through the potted palms.

CHAD FOUND BRITTANY alone in a side room, eating dinner in front of the Tampa Bay Buccaneer–Minnesota Viking football game, the sound turned on low. Either she had no interest in the game and the commentary, or she didn't want to turn the volume up loud enough for others to find her and drift inside, once again confirming that she wasn't interested in the men.

A brass chandelier lent the dark-paneled room a homey intimacy, as did flames crackling in a stone fireplace, scenting the room with pine. The maroon carpet was plush, the leather sofas Italian and butter soft, the gilt-framed art on the walls stunning replicas of Michelangelo's and Raphael's best works. The armoire, desk, and a cabinet set in various niches looked like they could have come right out of Versailles.

A beveled mirror over a lit stone fireplace caught his reflection, so he didn't startle her when he teased, "You aren't going to find Mr. Right on television."

"Bite me." Her two-word response shot like bullets, aimed to cut a man down or, at the very least, send him into a wounded, full-fledged retreat.

So the lady had a temper and didn't mind showing her claws. He could live with that. In fact, he'd be happy to respond by sinking his teeth into tender areas of her flesh. She certainly looked good enough to eat, with her silk blouse softly molding to her tense and very nibbleable shoulders, a touch of barbecue sauce on her cheek.

"Relax, Brittany. I only want to talk. I have a proposition for you."

"I'm *not* interested in being one of your women," she snapped.

"That's why I'm here," he admitted. He sat next to her on the sofa, thigh to thigh, and picked up her napkin. "You have a drop of sauce on your cheek."

He raised his hand with the napkin, hesitated, giving her every chance to pull back. She held perfectly still, eyes mesmerizingly alert and staring at him, unblinking. When he first brushed the napkin across her skin, his fingers grazed flesh firm and warm to the touch.

As if coming unfrozen, she yanked the napkin from his grasp and scooted back, almost knocking her dinner plate from her lap to the floor. She eyed him as if she didn't know whether to call for help or slap him. Instead, she placed the plate on the coffee table and roughly swiped away the sauce.

The television set caught her eye and she jumped to her feet. "Yes. Go. Go!"

Tampa's corner had recovered a fumble and was running the ball back from the Viking ten-yard line to the twenty, the thirty. Sacked at the fifty.

"All right. He's within Gramatica's leg range now." Her eyes shined with pleasure.

He helped himself to one of her untouched baby-back ribs. "You follow football?"

"I adore the game," she admitted, her eyes softening, glowing. For the first time he noticed how warm she could be once he penetrated her frosty facade.

"Where have you been all my life?" he asked, and when her eyes turned into chips of ice that didn't look about to thaw anytime this century, he realized he'd touched a nerve. Apparently, personal comments or compliments put her on the defensive. She was touchy. Very touchy.

"Up until now, I've been somewhere you weren't. Too bad that's changed."

Chad wasn't deterred. Since she liked football, and openly admitted it, he suspected she was a lot more down-to-earth than she let on. He couldn't resist teasing her, seeing if he could break down her defenses. "Well, since we both like football, I figure we'd be perfect together."

She actually laughed, her smile flashing the heat of

sunshine that warmed him straight to his toes. "Sure, right after the Tampa Bay Bucs win the Superbowl."

He helped himself to some coleslaw from her plate, pleased he'd put a dent in her detachment. "If you're from New York, why aren't you a Jets or a Giants fan?"

"I am," she admitted, her foot twitching as the Bucs' offense went three and out then called in the kicker to attempt a fifty-six yard field goal. "That's doable."

"It'd be his longest of the season, but he has the leg for it."

The kicker planted his foot. Kicked the ball straight through the goalposts, tying the game.

Brittany pumped her fist. "All right."

Chad watched her eyes light up with enthusiasm and wondered if she ever looked that happy unless her favorite teams were winning. "So when did you get to be a Tampa Bay fan?"

"My foundation coordinated a relief effort for the victims of Hurricane Andrew from the Tampa Bay area. I went to a few games to solicit donations and I got hooked."

Her gaze focused on the game, her lips softly parted. He knew how they'd taste. Lush. Slightly tangy from the barbecue sauce. Ripe with outrage if he dared kiss her.

During the two-minute warning of the fourth quarter, she flicked the channels, using the remote and upping the volume as a buffer to avoid conversation.

He polished off her sweet potatoes. "You never asked me why I'm interested in you."

"You fed me a line, I won't swallow the bait, and you won't reel me in." She gestured for him to leave. "Your time would be better spent with the others."

"You don't find me attractive?"

Her lips almost smiled, then she regained full control and pressed them into a firm line of dismissal. "That's not the point."

"You didn't answer the question."

"Back off, Chad." She lifted her chin, squared her shoulders like a soldier about to march into war and glared at him, but he sensed the effort it cost her. He'd gotten under her skin. Fortunately, since he'd grown up with six sisters, he knew quite well how to see right through a woman's brush-off attempts.

She'd overreacted because it wasn't easy for her to ignore him.

"Aha." He snapped his fingers and waggled his brows. "You want me to go away *because* you find me attractive."

She let out a weary sigh, but the fire kindling in her eyes told him she was anything but bored. "I find you intrusive. Egotistical."

"A man might call those same traits persistence and confidence."

"Then why don't you go find a *man* who appreciates you."

She crossed one leg over the other, clearly determined to freeze him out. He wasn't about to let that happen, enjoying the combination and contrast of fire and ice. Obviously she didn't care if he froze or burned.

He took the napkin from her and used a fresh corner to dab at his lips. "Sorry, I only like women, especially women who like football. Which leads me to why I'm here. I have a very important question to ask you."

She sighed. "What?"

He pointed his fork at the plate in front of him. "Are you going to eat this piece of cherry pie?"

She rolled her eyes. "I wouldn't want you to starve. Why don't you take it to go? I wouldn't mind at all."

He picked up her dessert and leaned back into the sofa, then used the fork to cut himself a generous bite of pie. "Not a chance. Not with two minutes left in the game and a tied score."

"Fine."

"Thanks for the warm invitation."

She speared him a fake smile.

When the Vikings snapped the ball, Brittany turned her attention back to the game, dismissing him, the frost in her eyes melting as she bit her bottom lip, waiting for action, trembling with the thrill of the game.

Cunningham stepped back in the pocket, launched a pass. Her lips parted in anticipation, her breath coming fast, furious, fevered. His mouth dried. Where would he have to touch her to elicit such passion? And precisely how?

The Bucs' All-Pro safety, John Lynch, intercepted, ran back for a touchdown.

Brittany jumped back to her feet in a giant release of tension and satisfaction. "Yes!"

The Bucs' kicker easily toed a field goal and Tampa Bay won by seven.

Chad was about to ask Brittany if she wanted to take a walk when Samantha strode into the room. She arched a brow at Chad. "I didn't expect to find you here with her."

He stood and glanced from Brittany to Samantha. Brittany looked as if she'd been caught in some risqué act. Samantha wasn't as easy to read. She fiddled nervously with a sash at her waist but walked toward him with a confident smile.

"Is there a problem, ma'am?" he asked.

"Nothing that can't be easily solved." Samantha possessively hooked her arm through Chad's. "I've purchased your services." Her gaze skewered Brittany. "Exclusively. For a month."

Chad swallowed, determined not to let her pronouncement shake him. He couldn't. He couldn't allow his disappointment to show in his face. He couldn't indicate in any way that he would have preferred Brittany to buy his contract. A hint of his irritation could be costly and dangerous to his mission.

Brittany stared at Samantha, her eyes wide with disdain and tinged with sorrow. She threw up her hands as she shook her head in disgust. "What the hell have you done?"

## 4

"BRITTANY," her mother used the soft-spoken tone that always set Brittany's teeth on edge. "For once in your life, don't think. Admit that you want him."

Chad looked from one woman to the other and frowned, his eyes clouded with confusion. Brittany saw no reason to spill the news that her mother had bought him for her daughter, since she found the matter embarrassing.

Brittany fisted her hands on her hips and glared, determined not to show her mother her conflicting emotions. She refused to look at the terribly roguish Chad Hunter and betray any hint of how incredibly charming she found him. *Charming* wasn't good enough. *Charming* reminded her of Devlin and of pain and betrayal. She'd counted on winning this bargain with her mother by avoiding any man who seemed the least bit interesting.

How like her mother to sense that not only did she find the SEAL attractive, he appealed to her in ways she didn't begin to understand. It wasn't just the way she responded to his physical attributes. A person was more than the sum of their parts—no matter how pleasing those parts. It was more than Chad's penetrating gaze or the way he *really* looked at her that had provoked her curiosity. It wasn't his height or his well-muscled limbs or even his easy grace wrapped around unadulterated power that caused her breath to catch in her throat whenever they locked gazes. It was more how she became so incredibly aware of his presence that made her very sure she didn't want to be alone with him—not even for a week, let alone for a whole month. Just one night could prove she hadn't conquered her weakness for charming men like her ex-husband, with their cocksure attitudes and teasing eyes.

That her mother had bought the one man in Eden that Brittany found difficult to ignore kindled her quiet anger into an out-of-control blaze. She was no longer an awkward kid at one of her mother's social extravaganzas, unable to speak her mind for fear of incurring Samantha's disapproval.

Trembling with annoyance, Brittany banked the fire and shot Samantha's clipped tone right back at her. "This time you've gone too far."

"Come on," her mother coaxed. "Tell me you feel the tiniest, dinkiest little bit of interest or I'll keep him all for myself."

"That's exactly what you should do. You keep him."

Stiff and obviously ill at ease, Chad removed his arm from Samantha's grasp. "Ladies, I'd rather rejoin the pool than come between your friendship."

"Not so fast." Samantha clasped Chad's hand to prevent him from leaving. "It's her decision." With a self-mocking raise of her eyebrow, her mother grinned at Chad. "Besides, you're not my type."

"And he's too…"

"Too what?" her mother challenged.

"Too…too…"

"Too much male for you?"

"Mother!"

Chad's jaw dropped as his eyes narrowed on Brittany. "Samantha Barrington's your mother?"

Brittany didn't look at Chad. She couldn't. Not with the heat flushing her face. "Despite the fact that I'm over twenty-one, she insists on treating me as if I'm sixteen."

"I'd hardly buy a man for my teenage daughter," Samantha said dryly.

Brittany saw Chad's eyes light up with understanding and amusement at her predicament, which made her even more determined to be rid of him. Of all the rotten luck, he had to be the man who'd caught Samantha's eye. Brittany had always been susceptible to a man's teasing, and Chad was no exception. No matter how aloof she tried to appear, a man who teased her seemed to slip right past her defensive barriers.

He folded his arms over his chest and demanded confirmation of her mother's plans. "You bought me for Brittany?"

Samantha nodded regally. "She likes you."

"I don't even know him," Brittany protested coolly. In reality she wanted to stomp her foot, throw a temper tantrum, then flee. She wouldn't give Samantha or Chad Hunter the satisfaction.

"I'll be good for her," Chad agreed and Brittany debated how hard a smack it would take to slap that delighted look off his face.

"No, you won't," she argued, but neither of them seemed to be listening.

"She's been hurt," Samantha added.

"I figured."

Brittany cut in. "Then you should be able to figure out that I don't appreciate being ignored." Wishing they'd quit talking as if she weren't there, Brittany stepped between them and fingered the top button of her blouse.

Chad noted the direction her hand had taken and seared her with a look hungry enough to make her mouth go dry. "I have no intention of ignoring you. Count on it."

Samantha chuckled and departed without another word. Brittany wanted the floor to open and swallow her, especially since Chad looked so smug—as if he'd chosen her, and her mother had had nothing to do with the arrangements.

"Look, I don't mean to be rude, but I don't want a man."

"Really?" He eyed her as she played with the button on her blouse again.

His skeptical tone made her stay firm, but an impish impulse caused her to continue to play with the button. "And I'm not changing my mind about us becoming intimately acquainted."

"So then what are you so fired up about? Who said you have to change your mind?"

What was he suggesting? She recalled him telling her he'd sought her out precisely because she wasn't interested. That made no sense, unless he wanted to earn a bonus without having sex. One look into his sexy eyes disabused her of that foolish notion. The man was made for lovemaking. Confidence oozed out of him with the air he exhaled. It was likely that Chad Hunter wanted a challenge, but she couldn't be sure of his thoughts any more than she could be sure of her reactions to him.

His questions threw her for a loop. Ever since her divorce, she'd avoided men by using a frosty attitude. After her past problems, she should want safety, security from a man. Anything but excitement. In Eden, her world had changed. Chad felt free to flirt with her, and she was responding in a way she would have before her marriage and divorce.

When Chad teased her, he slipped through her natural wariness, a wariness that had kept men at a distance. Why couldn't he understand the obvious? She didn't want the reminders that she'd once been warm and bold and unafraid. She now knew desire could lead to disaster. Did she have to spell out how embarrassing she found the entire situation, which was all the more uncomfortable because she found her flesh tingling with a need for his caress, her lips aching for a kiss?

Ignoring the blatant signals that her body was sending, she gestured to the sofa, took a seat and used the remote control to turn off the television. He joined her, looking so comfortably casual that she had the strongest urge to shake the complacency off his too-handsome face. After taking a deep breath, she forced her eyes to meet his and once again felt knocked back by the power of his glance, that air of confidence he wrapped about him like a cloak, as if he controlled all the space around him by his presence alone.

Determined to set him straight and define the terms of their relationship, she licked her bottom lip and eased into the subject gradually. "Mother thinks I work too much."

"Do you?" He focused on her mouth, seemingly fascinated by her tongue.

She refrained from licking her lip again and slicked back a stray lock of hair. "That's not the point. Samantha dragged me here against my will."

He arched a cynical eyebrow, his lips twitching as if he was trying to hold back laughter. "She kidnapped you?"

"Not exactly." Brittany didn't appreciate his kidding since her natural reaction to teasing was to let down her guard. Now she had to fight her response to him, battle her inclination to relax when she should be throwing up a higher wall. Explaining to a stranger was difficult enough without him trying to distract her with the sheer husky heat in his voice. Forcing the male aura he radiated from her mind was more difficult than she would have liked, but she focused her thoughts and stared at the logs burning in the fireplace, wondering where to begin and how to explain without sounding ridiculous.

"She bribed you to come here?" Chad guessed.

"Good guess."

"And her motive?"

"She claims motherly love."

He nodded. "She does seem concerned about your happiness."

"She's sticking her nose in my business." Brittany shrugged uncomfortably. She resented the need to talk about her wheeler-dealer mother with a stranger—especially a stranger who'd so recently promised that he would never ignore her. At the memory, she felt as if flames licked over her, raising her temperature by several degrees.

Chad's offer had been more enticing than she wanted to admit. It had been so very long since she'd last made love to a man—so very long since she'd allowed herself to be naked and vulnerable. Which was exactly the reason her wily mother had brought Brittany to Eden and exactly why she'd bought Chad Hunter's contract.

Brittany reminded herself Eden wasn't the real world. In Eden, she was in charge. She was calling the shots. She had the power to decide how far she wanted to go. As Chad had so astutely pointed out, she didn't have to change her mind about being intimate with him. Therefore she had no reason to be upset by the way his teasing got under her skin and invaded her thoughts...since she had no intention of sleeping with him.

CHAD WATCHED BRITTANY finger the button where the smooth V of flesh at her neck met enticing silk. He wondered if her gesture was deliberately provocative. Was she testing him? Was she one of those women who needed to be coaxed and cajoled? A woman who couldn't enjoy a man unless he talked her into making love? He couldn't be positive, but the labels didn't quite fit. At one moment she seemed so sure of herself, the next she retreated behind a wall of ice that froze him out.

While her outward inconsistencies intrigued him, he also had to figure out the best way to deal with her. She was so good at keeping men at a distance with a cool look, a disinterested expression or cold body language. Yet she had occasionally let down her guard. He had to figure out exactly what caused the reaction he wanted—and do it again.

Meanwhile, he kept his antennae up. Should he be suspicious that Brittany fit so well into his plans? He didn't suspect her of duplicity, since her mother had arranged their match, but he thought it mighty convenient that he'd so easily achieved exactly what he wanted. With Brittany to escort about, he would soon have more freedom to search the premises for Lyle. She wouldn't demand too much of his personal services in return, but if she didn't stop fingering that damn button soon, he couldn't be held responsible if he stole a kiss or two.

He reminded himself he was here on a mission. The setup was perfect. Maybe too perfect. Then again, perhaps he had just lucked out.

Clearly Brittany's mother and the ex-judge knew each other well. Did they suspect he'd come to Eden under false pretenses? Had they intentionally set him up with Brittany to give him enough rope to hang himself?

Or was Chad seeing conspiracies where none existed? He reminded himself that no matter Brittany's seeming coolness to him, he needed her to keep him around, which meant walking a razor-fine edge between provoking her interest, encouraging her curiosity and stopping her retreat into the igloo she seemed to live in most of the time.

"Why don't you tell me exactly what you want?" he asked as gently and as reasonably as he could, letting his eyes reveal how much he liked what he saw.

Primly she crossed one long leg over the other. The chips of ice in her eyes would have frostbitten a less determined man. She tilted her elegant neck at an aristocratic angle, her profile clearly sending signals that read *hands off*. "I want to be alone."

"That's not going to happen." By her frosty expression, he could tell his answer irritated her, but also seemed to shake her out of her complacency. He shot her his most charming good-guy smile. "You don't want to admit that you like me?"

When she ignored his statement, he restrained a grin. He was getting to her. He knew it when she licked her bottom lip again. Was teasing the key to melting the ice around her?

"I should send you away."

Her tongue darted over lush lips and made him all too aware that this conversation was taking place on several levels—including an emotional and a physical one. She'd said she *should* send him away, but she hadn't followed through, which meant that while she might still be resisting, she was losing an inner battle. As if clearly determined to meet him head-on, she eyeballed him with a touch of aloofness. He wanted to break through, but he needed to be careful not to push her too hard.

"If you dismiss my services, your mother would replace me, and you'd have to start over with someone else."

"You have a point." Her eyes turned bold. Provocative. "But if I can't be alone, maybe someone else might be more to my liking."

"Perhaps." He was walking a very fine line. He wanted to charm her, intrigue her, dare her to stand up to him. So far she'd responded to him and she seemed to be enjoying the challenge even if she wasn't willing to admit it. Right now his mission was to convince her that while she had the upper hand, he was the man who could hold her interest. He took a gamble and teased her again, "I don't think you have any idea what you want."

In a gesture he found both temptingly brazen and endearingly sweet, she wagged a finger at him. "And, of course, *you* know what I want."

"Oh, yeah." He focused on her bottom lip before raising his gaze to meet hers. "And what you want is very different from what you need."

She rolled her eyes at the ceiling.

He didn't let her disdain stop him, not since he'd made a pin-sized hole in the block of ice. "You want me to keep my distance."

"By George, you've finally got it."

He hoped he wasn't pushing her too far, but from the fervor of her last statement, he suspected she was both enjoying and getting irritated by his comments. She liked being teased. "But you need me."

Her hazel eyes frothed like a stormy sea. "Why do men always presume they are experts at what women need?"

"Why do you presume I'm not?"

"Don't you think I know my own mind?"

"Do you?"

With a shake of her head, she shoved to her feet. "This isn't going to work."

"Because you won't let it work."

"It's my fault?" She sounded incredulous.

"Look. I started this conversation by asking you a very specific question about what you wanted."

"I don't owe you explanations."

"True. But you don't play fair." He switched gears quickly, wondering if he'd stepped over the line with his teasing and if he could backpedal.

She frowned, her mouth a pretty pout that begged to be kissed. "What do you mean?"

"How would you like to be hired for a job and then not be told what's expected?"

She didn't say a word. Instead she strode to the fireplace, giving him time to admire her back. She had delicate shoulders, squared to do battle, which narrowed to a trim waist, a waist slender enough for his hands to span. She walked, her hips swaying with a femininity that teased and taunted him into imagining what she wore beneath—silk, cotton, or nothing at all? He imagined that she was quite annoyed with him, but there was an innate honesty about her that told him she would be fair. That fairness would compel her to go further than she'd contemplated.

Unless he guessed wrong and she dumped him. With another woman, he would have stood, maybe taken her into his arms and tried to persuade her with soft words murmured into her ear, a gentle caress of her back, maybe the lightest of kisses. Brittany wasn't ready for kisses. She wasn't ready for his touch. In fact, she barely deigned to look directly at him, instead often talking to a point beyond his right shoulder.

So he gave her the room she required. Waited. Held his breath while she drew out the moment, putting another log on the fire, using an iron to shove the wood into the flames. Finally she whirled around, her face flushed from the heat of the fire, her eyes bright with intensity. "Let's start over. I'll tell you exactly what I want."

He wondered if she knew how cute she looked all fired up with determination. He laced his fingers behind his head and leaned back into the sofa. "I'm listening."

"We'll spend the month together as…companions."

"Companions?" He tried to make his voice sound slightly disappointed and found it wasn't difficult. The longer he spent with her, the more attractive he found her. The way she fingered the button on her blouse whenever she was nervous tempted him to provoke her. The way she licked her lip when she turned bold was downright fascinating and would undoubtedly haunt his dreams tonight—that is, if he got to sleep at all.

She raised a brow. "We won't make love."

"Are you sure you'll be able to keep your hands off me?" he teased, loving the sparks that flared in her eyes.

"Somehow I'll manage to keep my hands to myself. We'll attend the planned activities and pretend to be lovers."

"Kissing might be required, then?" he asked, wondering how she would deal with his question, daring her once again to go further than she'd intended.

She nodded, lips pressed tight. "Are we agreed?"

"Sure. There's only one thing." He stood, approached her and cupped her chin, enjoying the smooth, velvety skin contrasting with the scowl of her lips.

"What?"

"If you want me to kiss you in public, we should practice in private first."

She chuckled, confidence sparkling. "I wouldn't think you'd need practice."

"*I* don't."

She flipped her hair over her shoulder. "Are you implying that I need practice?"

"Yeah. I need to know how you'll respond before I kiss you in public."

"Why?"

He shrugged and moved closer until he could distinguish the green ring around her pupils. "I could explain." He dropped his lips to within an inch of hers. "But it's so much more fun to show you."

She didn't retreat, didn't move back. "I'm not interested in *fun*. I want you to obey my rules so we can get through the month."

"You object to enjoying yourself?"

"I won't enjoy your kiss."

"Oh, I won't enjoy it, either," he teased. "In fact, I'm going to have to force myself to do my job." He whispered, his lips so close to hers they were a fraction of an inch from touching. "But no matter how unpleasant, I'm trained to be thorough."

Her pupils dilated, the black centers expanding to encompass the green rings, leaving only a hint of soulful brown iris calling to the devil in him. He wondered if she realized that at the last moment, she leaned into him, or that by remaining silent, she caused his pulse to beat double time.

Ever so slowly, he dipped his head until he breathed in the tangy scent of barbecue mixed with the spicy aroma of lip gloss, giving her every opportunity to retreat from his advance. She held perfectly still, and that was all the encouragement he required. He nibbled at the corner of her lush lips, knowing he would consider his strategy a victory if he could persuade her lips to part for him.

He ached to place his arms around her back, nestle her against his chest. He wanted to thread his fingers through her hair and revel in exploring the quiet texture of her. Sweet anticipation filled his taste buds, but he held back, content to nibble on her lower lip and let his fingers trace a greedy path down her spine.

He would wait. Wait until she demanded more.

BRITTANY KNEW she should put an immediate halt to his kiss. She seemed frozen on the slippery edge of a giant chasm unable to climb upward, unable to let go for fear of sliding into a bottomless pit where she might never emerge. Chad's mesmerizing eyes pinned her, dared her, and she found herself wanting. Wanting more. Wanting him. A wanting that had begun during their conversation when he'd deliberately teased and provoked her. She'd protested as a matter of course, but she hadn't been able to suppress the very feminine heat that coursed through her veins and caused her blood to simmer and her breasts to swell with a delicious tingle.

Damn the man! He hadn't let up, relentless with his bedroom eyes, his provocative tone, his arrogant charm. She didn't want to know him. She didn't want to like him. And she certainly didn't want to want him.

*It's just lust. A kiss won't hurt.*

In fact, his kiss couldn't possibly match her expectations. Devlin had been the world's best kisser. Her ex had been a wonderful lover. She didn't think another man could live up to the memories of her first love.

Chad's kiss couldn't possibly be potent enough to make her forget that she planned for them to remain platonic companions. He was bound to disappoint her, the lust would subside, and she would regain control of her galloping emotions.

All she need do was stand there, refuse to respond to him and flush any ideas of romance out of her system. No kiss was irresistible. No kiss would blind her to the reality that she didn't want a physical relationship. No kiss would make her forget that she was here for only a month and then she'd never see Chad Hunter again.

She expected the powerful SEAL to sweep her into his arms, but his touch was so delicate, so whisper light that she had to concentrate to feel his lips exploring hers. Just the slightest brush of his mouth caused an involuntary tremble and an ache that slipped behind her defenses.

Prepared for a full-fledged assault, she was unprepared for his sneak attack that left her wanting more. In absolutely no hurry, he nipped and nibbled her bottom lip and nuzzled her jaw while his fingers lightly stroked her back in slow, sensual circles. She breathed in the masculine scent of him mixed with cherry pie, and a small sigh escaped her throat. A kiss might just be a kiss, but Chad's kisses were magic. He'd flown her to heaven on a flying carpet of pure, exotic bliss.

It took every ounce of control not to raise her hands

to his head and draw him to her. She'd closed her eyes, but a flutter of his lashes against her cheek caused her to look at him. His breath was even while hers had turned ragged. That he was enjoying himself, she had no doubts. The heat in his eyes should have made her wary, but instead it kindled an answering spark inside her that she couldn't put out and that flared into an inferno of need.

When his mouth again brushed hers, she parted her lips, welcoming him and telling herself she would only be in Eden for a month and she might as well enjoy some of it. Why not loosen up and enjoy a man's attentions for a change? After all, once the month was up, she'd probably never see Chad again anyway.

She wanted more, not a mere hint, she wanted the full measure of the man. A husky growl from the back of his throat caused her to lean into him and savor the pleasure that started at her mouth and sizzled straight to her toes.

"I hope you aren't having any *fun*," he whispered into her mouth.

She could barely think through the sensual web of passion he'd woven around her. "Why?"

"Because then I would have to stop kissing you."

"I don't think I'm having fun yet," she murmured, realizing she'd just given him permission to keep kissing her, unable to deprive herself.

Chad Hunter definitely knew how to kiss. He didn't rush, he didn't press. He seemed to enjoy discovering exactly what she liked and then giving it to her in doses so small she ached impatiently for more.

And when her legs trembled so that she thought she might lose her balance, his strong, clever hands steadied her, his broad chest supported her. In the security of his arms, she forgot everything except the sensations coursing through her like a heat wave.

She found herself with her arms wrapped around his neck, her breasts pressed tight to his chest, taking everything he gave her.

Taking his warmth.

Learning his heartbeat.

Soaking up his taste.

In an amazingly few minutes, he'd swept her to a place where she hadn't been in a long time—perhaps not ever. As much as she wanted to tell herself she'd responded to Chad Hunter because she hadn't made love in several long years, as much as she wanted to believe this was simple lust, she knew better.

Lust wouldn't leave her shaken to the foundation of her soul. Lust wouldn't leave her so fearful of making a huge mistake.

She'd felt these kinds of sizzling emotions before—with Devlin. He, also, had known how to kiss her. He had sparked a desire in her that had grown into passion, then love. She'd been so sure their marriage would last a lifetime. She'd been wrong, and she refused to make the same mistake again.

Planting a palm on Chad's chest, she pulled back, more breathless than she wanted to admit. "I think that we've practiced enough."

# 5

"THERE YOU ARE, Brittany." Samantha separated from a group of men and women talking near the barbecue grills and welcomed Brittany with a smile. "I'm so proud of you, dear."

Her mother's compliment almost stopped Brittany in her tracks. After Chad's bone-melting kiss, she had yet to regain her equilibrium. She'd fled, muttering some excuse, leaving him in the television room and rejoining the group by the buffet. She'd had only one goal in mind—self-preservation, which meant sending Chad back to the pool of men and breaking the deal with her mother.

"You're proud of me?" Brittany parroted, knowing she needed to pull herself together. A kiss shouldn't have rattled her so. She'd pegged Chad for a charmer, but she'd never expected one kiss to change her perception of Eden. Before she'd come to the resort, she'd considered the idea of buying a man's services repugnant. Now...all she could think about was that spectacular kiss and how much she already craved another. She wondered if power could corrupt her so easily. Or if she could already be addicted.

"Of course I'm proud of you. You're holding up your end of the bargain." Her mother stirred the ice in her drink with a perfectly manicured finger while she squinted, her gaze centered on Brittany's mouth.

"Is my lip gloss smudged?" Although Brittany had made a mad dash in retreat from Chad, she'd stopped in the ladies' room to brush her hair and apply fresh makeup.

"Your lips…look…it's nothing."

Brittany recognized the gleam in Samantha's eyes, the one she saved for special triumphs. Raising her finger to her mouth, Brittany realized her lips were slightly swollen and her mother had guessed the reason. Chad's kiss.

That the evidence was so apparent caused a rush of heat to her face. If her mother had noticed, she was too diplomatic to comment, but Brittany took a moment to regroup and lost her opportunity for a private conversation.

"Ah, Brittany dear." Laurel rolled up in her wheelchair, unlit cigar in hand. "I do believe your SEAL meat is the tastiest-looking filet I've ever seen—charbroiled on the outside and tender inside."

How would Laurel know what Chad was like on the inside? How does anyone ever know? Brittany wondered. She'd been married to Devlin for almost two years, and she hadn't known the man at all. She'd thought he was perfect—right up to the day she'd walked in on him with another woman.

Brittany wished she had time to be alone, to reassess that kiss, to think about how best to deal with

Chad. She didn't dare let Laurel and her mother catch her woolgathering. If they realized Chad's kiss had knocked her socks off—or would have if she'd been wearing any—there was no telling what mischief they would create. So Brittany took a deep breath, forced Chad's kiss from her mind and concentrated on her surroundings.

Laurel wore a rhinestone-studded T-shirt, matching rhinestone jeans and cowboy boots with yet more of her signature rhinestones. Brittany wondered if the woman had dressed early for the masquerade planned for later this evening, but didn't dare ask for fear of insulting her mother's eccentric friend.

Irritated but accustomed to Laurel's assessment of men, and frustrated by the ex-judge's presence, which prevented her from trying to back out of the bargain with her mother, Brittany pasted a smile on her face as Chad joined the ladies. He positioned himself close to her and took her hand as if she belonged to him and not the other way around. His gesture should have annoyed her, but she couldn't deny the pleasure of his strong fingers gently wrapping around hers any more than the effect he was having on her emotions.

"Ladies." Chad greeted Laurel and her mother with an affable nod. He didn't seem the least discombobulated by their kiss. He didn't look as if someone had taken all his emotions and stirred them to a boil. Quite the contrary, Chad Hunter looked calm and collected until he turned his hungry eyes on Brittany.

Her raw emotions swung the gamut from sweet fear to full-fledged panic to lust so powerful she trembled.

The cycle kept escalating, spiraling in an upward succession of anxiety, confusion and passion that had her dizzy trying to sort out exactly what she wanted. This state of bewilderment was unsettling her, and while she deliberated upon her next course of action, Chad had already made his move.

"If you'll excuse us." Chad gently tugged on Brittany's arm. "We need to choose costumes for the masquerade."

Samantha's hand on his arm stopped their departure. "I already picked out your outfits."

"Mother!" Was Samantha leaving nothing to chance?

Laurel clamped down on her cigar, her multitude of rhinestones flashing almost blindingly. "Don't worry. Your costumes are exquisite. I helped Samantha pick them out." Brittany held back a groan.

As Laurel considered Chad's backside, he quickly led Brittany away and whispered in her ear, "Think there's any chance they'll be…decent?"

"I'd settle for legal," Brittany complained. "While my mother's taste is impeccable—" she shuddered slightly "—with Laurel egging her on, we might find ourselves decked out in rhinestones and little else."

"That might not be so bad."

"Yeah, well, just remember that it's not my butt that Laurel's after."

Chad shot her a dangerous smile. "No problem. I'll tell her that from now on…my ass belongs to you."

ALL THE FESTIVITIES were conveniently located in the same area as the barbecue. The ladies had their own private rooms upstairs where they could relax, shower and change for the masquerade. The men didn't need to return to their area to don costumes since a changing area had been provided. Many of the ladies had yet to make their choices, and the men without exclusive contracts had the advantage of picking out their own costumes.

Employees directed Chad and several other men, including Francois, the uninhibited dancer that the model Aurora had put under contract, to a separate and more private area where preselected costumes hung on a rack, name tags pinned to the costumes.

Francois accepted his pirate costume with a happy grin. "My Aurora appreciates the finer things in life. Yes?"

"She certainly chose *you* in a hurry," Chad agreed.

"The best are always chosen first," Francois told him with an immodest grin. "And this costume shall make me irresistible."

Chad took the opportunity of waiting in line to check out the surveillance equipment. As in every area of the resort, he saw web cams, security guards and video cameras. When one of the attendants handed Chad a costume, he didn't pay much attention to his evening attire, instead focusing on Francois's chatter, waiting for the man to pause so he could insert a question.

Finally Chad got his chance. "You hear of any other SEALs in Eden?"

"Lyle Gates came through here a few months back. A friend of yours?"

"It's a small arm of the navy, but we're scattered all over the world." Chad didn't outright lie, but left out information by omission and misdirection. He shrugged, trying to appear casual, telling himself to be careful and not ask too many questions.

"Well, this SEAL got snapped up right way just like we did. I heard there was some kind of accident." Francois paused and, when Chad remained silent, he continued. "He ended up in the infirmary."

"Eden seems safe enough to me." Chad took some kind of green vest off the hangar. In addition he saw a turban and tight-waisted black pants that flared at the thighs and knees before cuffing around the ankles. Where was the shirt?

An attendant tapped him on the shoulder. "Sorry, sir. This part of your costume got mixed up with another." Chad turned, expecting to see his missing shirt. Instead, the attendant pressed a fake beard into his hand.

Francois waited until after the other man departed. "Anyway, the story goes that Laurel caught the SEAL going out her window to meet another woman. And then...Lyle Gates ended up in the hospital."

"There's a hospital in Eden?" Chad asked, putting it at the top of his list of places to check out.

"Aren't you curious about what happened to him?"

Francois looked at him oddly, and Chad realized he'd been playing it too cautiously. It was natural to ask questions. After all, whatever had happened to Lyle could happen to them.

"I assume he recovered. It's hard to keep a good SEAL down."

"Was that a boast?"

"A fact."

Chad knew the other man was making a sexual innuendo about his comment and let it go. This was his first real clue to Lyle's disappearance. Knowing Laurel had bought him and that he'd ended up in the hospital where there had to be medical records caused Chad's mind to hum. Before too long, he would make sure he visited the hospital. He doubted the information he wanted would be left in the open, and he'd prefer to explore the hospital on a legitimate visit, then return later once he'd scoped out the layout and security.

Tonight he would be moving into Brittany's quarters. Since he assumed they wouldn't be sharing a bed, he should have ample opportunity for reconnaissance.

BRITTANY TOOK ONE look at her harem-girl costume and sighed. She supposed she should be glad the bra-like emerald top with green sequins and the tiny bottom covered the essentials. Long gauzy pants that would reveal her legs didn't do much to comfort her either. Although she supposed the costume wasn't any more revealing than her swimsuit, she wasn't going swimming.

As she donned the fanciful costume, she imagined

what Chad would be wearing. Would she be playing harem girl to his sheik? At least those long robes would cover Chad's magnificent body and help keep her mind on simply getting through the evening.

A knock on her private room was followed by Samantha's breezy entrance. "Hi, dear."

Her mother wore more clothes than Brittany had expected. Dressed as a hippie, she had chosen a tie-dyed T-shirt with Peter Max's signature American flag, love beads and jeans artfully torn at knee and thigh by her favorite designer. Apparently her mother had decided to go barefoot, too.

Brittany turned around and tried to tug up the low-slung, hip-hugging bottoms that insisted on remaining two inches below her naval. "I'm going to freeze."

"Chad will keep you warm," her mother insisted as she reached into her handbag and took out makeup.

"So who's your date?" Brittany asked, changing the subject.

"I'm still looking."

Brittany wondered if her mother was still pining for the sculptor Jeffrey Payne. She didn't ask. She'd only been glad when the pain haunting her mother's eyes had lifted, replaced by her old sparkle. Since her mother seemed back to her former self, Brittany wouldn't bring up the hurtful subject.

She also didn't see the point of having so much skin showing. With her top designed as one of those push-up bras in disguise, she had enough cleavage to feel like a fraud.

Her mother placed a gentle hand on her shoulder. "Sit."

Brittany knew the drill. She sat. Her mother was an absolute whiz with makeup and wouldn't be deterred. Samantha had given up fighting the small battles long ago and saved her energy to win the war.

"Want to switch costumes?" she asked, knowing her mother expected her to complain. If she didn't, Samantha might suspect that Brittany didn't mind the brief costume—and that would be giving away too much of her feelings. Brittany had started to think it wouldn't hurt to let loose a little and have a good time tonight.

Samantha shook her head as she applied eye shadow with a steady hand. "Your costume matches Chad's. He's a genie."

"A genie?" Despite her best effort, Brittany couldn't quite envision what he'd look like, but several minutes later, when they entered the masquerade ball, she spotted him immediately and her mouth went dry.

Amid several hundred men and women swirling across the dance floor, and under a flickering globe that splashed shimmering lights on the costumed party goers who stood talking in intimate groups, Chad stood out like a beacon. He looked good in a beard—but then he looked good period.

Most of the men were fairly well covered, dressed as pirates and spacemen and cowboys. Chad's costume didn't have as much material as the others. In fact, only a skimpy green vest covered his tanned chest. His flat stomach and feet were as bare as hers, although his legs were decently hidden by black pants.

Music swirled around them and the bounce in her step made her ponytail dance. And she suddenly knew why she hadn't protested much over this costume. She'd wanted Chad to see her and admire her.

What the hell was wrong with her? She didn't dress to please men, but to please herself. She preferred to blend in, and although she'd allowed Samantha to choose some of her clothes to wear in Eden as part of their deal, she hadn't dressed to draw a man's attention since her divorce. Yesterday, she'd stood next to Aurora just so men wouldn't notice her. Now she was going to flaunt her body before Chad like a tasty meal.

She touched her lips, wondering what his kiss had done to her. Suddenly she saw nothing wrong with enjoying a man's attention for a change. She'd kept herself at her desk for too many months and now that she was here, she intended to live a little. It wasn't men who interested her—just one man and his reactions. As she joined Chad, she barely noticed the appreciative glances of other men.

She had eyes only for Chad and let her gaze feast on him. His genie costume showed off appetizing muscles that were smooth and taut like an Olympic swimmer's. A powerful neck and broad shoulders that mountained down to his chest made her mouth water with appreciation. Her mother had been right. She wasn't cold at all. In fact, she felt warm, her bones feeling like hot caramel.

"You look terrific," he told her, leaning forward and planting a casual kiss on her cheek. His turban tilted at an angle.

She reached up to straighten it. "Careful."

"So are you going to give me a hint? Who are you this evening?"

"Your harem girl." She laughed to show him she wasn't serious. "Laurel and Samantha's little joke. Don't take it too seriously."

"Of course not. I don't want you to have too much fun," he teased. "Would you mind telling me exactly what I'm supposed to be?"

"A genie."

His eyes widened. "Like out of the bottle?"

"Like the kind that grants three wishes."

He drew her into a private alcove, with a window seat and a bay window that overlooked a garden. "Three wishes. Now that sounds...enticing." He stood close, his voice husky. "Have you decided on your wishes?"

What she really wanted was another kiss, but she wouldn't admit it for all the bonbons in Paris. "Let's just have a good time."

"But not too much fun?"

"Exactly." She met his eyes in the dim light, grateful that he couldn't see a blush rising up her neck, pleased he didn't push her. Then hypocritically, she had to suppress a small quiver of disappointment that he so easily allowed her to set limits.

"And your second wish?"

"I'll need some time to consider."

"I don't think so."

"Excuse me?"

"You don't need more time. You need more courage. You're simply afraid to ask." The words were both gentle and bold and dead-on accurate. When had he gotten to know her so well? Was she that transparent? Once, a long time ago, she had had the courage to live boldly, and she suddenly wanted to reclaim that part of herself. Perhaps, tonight, with Chad's help, she could.

"Be gentle with me."

"Always." His eyes kindled and flared with the hot look she'd been wanting to see earlier when he'd noticed her body clad in the provocative costume. This reaction was much more personal and much more difficult to resist. However his approval gave her the courage to murmur her last wish—even knowing it revealed her vulnerability.

She took both his hands in hers, faced him, standing tall in her bare feet, shoulders squared. "Promise you won't ever lie to me."

At her request, she thought perhaps she saw the tiniest hint of concern there before deciding she must have been mistaken. In the moonbeam shining through the alcove's window, the light wasn't good enough to read such subtleties.

"Your wish is my command." His words were light and, as he touched her bare back, a hot shiver spiked down her spine. He led her from the alcove's privacy. "Would you like to dance?"

Her pulse pounded as they joined the other couples on the dance floor, her feet already tapping to the rock-and-roll beat. "You're very well-rounded for a military man."

"You can thank my sisters for my light feet. Mine were the toes they stepped on while they practiced for homecoming and senior prom."

"Then you're a good dancer?"

"I have six sisters." He escorted her onto the parquet with a cocky grin. "But I'll let you be the judge."

CHAD DANCED with the grace of a jungle cat on the prowl, keeping perfect cadence to the beat, automatically timing his steps so they moved as a couple. Like some wild creature, his eyes constantly perused the crowd, watching, judging. Searching? Brittany couldn't help wondering if she had his full attention.

He did nothing overt like flirt with other women. He smiled at the right times, guided her to a roomier spot when other dancers happened to encroach in their space. Yet she had the distinctly uncomfortable impression that despite Chad's expertise, he wasn't into the dancing.

It had been a long two days. Eden's founders kept experts on staff to plan the mixers, barbecue and masquerade. The entire month was filled with activities that provided the women and men ample opportunity to take full advantage of meeting and socializing.

Some events were formal, others casual. In addition, the lush resort provided all the amenities, from restaurants to sailing on the lake to special rooms where couples shared private fantasies—rooms Brittany planned to avoid.

While Samantha had warned her the first days were always the most stressful, Brittany thought she was beginning to know Chad well enough to realize when he was distracted. Then again, perhaps her insecurities were showing. Was he dissatisfied with their bargain? Did he regret being tied to her for a month?

She certainly wouldn't have thought so by the heat of his kiss. Reminding herself that the man had likely gotten to be an expert due to a lot of practice with other women did nothing to cool the sparks he'd fanned deep in her belly. No amount of rationalization could convince her that he'd felt nothing during their kiss. It wasn't possible for only one person to feel fireworks shooting off sky-high while the other stayed grounded.

Chad certainly knew the right moves. He was all male animal, light on his feet, touching her shoulder, her hip, her back. Maybe it was a coincidence that, when he spied Laurel, he maneuvered them to the crowd's edge, near to where the ex-judge was holding court with her cronies.

"How about a drink?" Chad asked Brittany.

"A glass of white wine, please."

Chad took her hand and they threaded through the costumed crowd to the open bar. He ordered their drinks, and Aurora and Francois joined Brittany.

Francois looked dashing in his pirate costume. He wore a flowing white shirt, black pants, boots and a patch over one eye. A sheathed sword at his side complemented his costume. However, it was Aurora who stunned Brittany. The model wore the female equivalent of a pirate's costume. Her white shirt tied under her breasts left her minuscule midriff bare. Instead of pants, she wore a postage-stamp-sized skirt and black, thigh-high boots. What surprised Brittany the most was the ugly fake scar that trailed from her eye to her chin. Apparently, Aurora had no qualms about marring her beauty.

"Having a good time?" Brittany asked.

"It's going to get better." Aurora winked at Francois. "I reserved the Ravishment Room for the evening."

From the passionate glances they shared, Brittany wasn't sure who would be ravishing whom. She didn't want to know. The couple seemed totally comfortable together and yet there was an eager anticipation, a sexual tension arcing between them that seemed at odds with their having met only hours ago.

Chad joined them and handed Brittany a glass of wine. "Did I hear you've reserved the Ravishment Room?" he asked Aurora.

"It's my favorite," she admitted, her eyes lighting with pleasure.

Francois put his arm over her shoulder. "Then I'm sure it will be my favorite, too."

The cooing couple made Brittany uncomfortable. It was as if she found herself lacking but wasn't sure how or why. She sipped her wine, grateful when the other couple left them for the dance floor.

She eyed Chad's clear drink with a lime and assumed he'd ordered a gin and tonic. When he leaned close to her ear, she didn't detect any liquor on his breath. "I was hoping for a slow dance next."

She didn't want him to see that the idea of him holding her close while they swayed to a slow song caused her pulse to quicken even as her mind told her she could handle the contact. When Chad downed his drink in one long swallow, she raised a questioning eyebrow.

"Club soda," he answered her unspoken question. "Dancing always leaves me thirsty."

As a song ended, the crowd stopped dancing and applauded, then the lights softened and slowed. Chad took her almost finished glass of wine and deposited both glasses on a nearby table. Before she knew quite how smoothly he'd maneuvered her, she was back on the dance floor.

He gathered her to him, swaying thigh to thigh, hip to hip, chest to chest, his palm on her bare back keeping her right where he wanted her. Close. So close her breasts tingled and her nipples hardened at the contact. So close that her thighs trembled with a weakness she couldn't control. So close she had trouble remembering she had any clothes on at all.

She'd never been skin to skin with Chad, not even when they'd shared that delectable kiss. Although they were in public, she could feel every hard inch of him, every muscle flexing, every beat of his heart.

It might have been a long time since she'd made love, but it wasn't so long that she'd forgotten how good it could be. She wanted to know Chad better. She wanted to taste the flavor of his skin where his neck met his shoulder, nip the muscle flexing there, hear him groan with need.

For a moment, she allowed herself to go with the flow, letting him lead her across the dance floor in smooth, graceful steps while she closed her eyes and tried to regain her senses. She'd been down that road before, had cravings that led to calamity. One glass of wine shouldn't have lowered her inhibitions anywhere near enough to be thinking such thoughts. Yet her blood seemed intoxicated, her mind almost numb.

How could she think with the clean masculine scent of him in every breath? The full-body contact of the dance was creating enough friction to shoot her up in flames and had her maneuvering to maintain an inch of air between them. She wriggled back, but he advanced, almost as if he were her second skin.

He held her left hand in his right, and she pressed her other hand against his shoulder and tilted her head back, intending to ask him to give her some breathing room. After she looked up, she thought she caught him off guard, focusing on someone across the dance floor. When he noticed her trying to follow his gaze, he shifted his focus to her.

"What's wrong?" she asked.

"Nothing." He smiled down at her without the slightest hint of embarrassment as his distinctive bulge brushed her hips. He wanted her, which made his next seeming distraction all the more difficult to explain.

He suddenly increased the pace of his steps, paying no attention to matching the music's rhythm for the first time all evening. They were weaving in and out of other couples, cutting off a magician and his assistant, spinning around a king and queen.

When they reached the far edge of the dance floor, Chad broke contact. "Excuse me. I have to use the rest room."

He abandoned her seemingly without a second thought, merged into the crowd, not once looking back. Baffled, flustered and disappointed, she waited impatiently for him to return.

Ten minutes later, with no sign of Chad, Brittany asked a man dressed in a devil's costume to check the rest room, fearing that Chad might be ill. How sick could he have been and still be sexually aroused?

The devil returned, a worried look on his face. "He's not there, ma'am. You want me to call security?"

# 6

CHAD HURRIED toward Brittany, overhearing the devil's suggestion and arriving in time to head off trouble. "There you are." He placed a hand on Brittany's shoulder and she jumped. "I've been looking for you."

Her eyes narrowed, her lips set in a firm line of disapproval, Brittany's suspicions were clearly written on her face. The warm woman dancing in his arms had been replaced by the ice queen, and her reaction was out of proportion to his having been missing for only ten minutes. Chad had no doubts he could thaw her, even if she'd seen more than she should have. After the way she had responded to him on the dance floor, she had to be having more good thoughts than she was willing to reveal.

Brittany shrugged out from under Chad's hand on her shoulder, her body language telling him he would have to work his way back into her good graces. The devil departed, the eddies and swirls of the crowd flowing around them. He might be swimming against an undercurrent of suspicion, but Chad knew how to angle his way to safety. First he needed a chance to explain. The music had once again returned to rock and roll, thundering in his ears, the dancing more frenetic, the crowd more raucous and the overhead spotlights blinking with blinding luminescence.

He took Brittany's elbow and guided her toward the nearest exit, the one he'd used to come in and hoped she hadn't seen. If necessary, he had a plan B for that contingency.

Experience with working on an undercover mission told him that the best lies were the simple ones. Unfortunately, he wouldn't be able to keep his promise to tell her only the truth for even the span of one night. He regretted the need for secrecy, didn't like the deception. However, even a large twinge of guilt wouldn't prevent him from doing his job.

Finding Lyle had to come first. While dancing with Brittany earlier, he'd spotted a masked man in the crowd who'd looked a lot like Lyle Gates. From across the room he couldn't be sure of a positive identification, but the man possessed Lyle's height, his muscular frame, his military bearing and his distinctive white-blond hair.

Wanting to get closer, Chad had danced Brittany across the floor. He still didn't know if the man he suspected was Lyle had recognized him, but as he'd closed in, the masked man had practically bolted for the door, leaving Chad no option but to make his excuse and pursue.

Those few seconds had cost him.

Chad had quickly slipped through the crowd as stealthily as possible, but his clever prey proved elusive. He'd disappeared, merging into the night shadows as if he'd never existed. The masked man's ability to avoid detection increased Chad's suspicion he was on Lyle's trail. SEALs were trained to move through the night without detection, to blend with the shadows, to become one with the darkness. All without uttering a sound or betraying their location by even taking a breath—like the man he was stalking.

Chad had tailed his quarry to a manicured garden of tall hedges, giant oak and maple trees, abundant flowers and twisting brick paths. He immediately lost sight of the dark silhouette. Even the knowledge that his mark had the advantage of a familiar territory didn't make him consider turning back.

While the masked man might have been innocently meeting a lover or simply taking a stroll in the night air, Chad had a hunch that the man had recognized him across the dance floor, then vanished. Lyle was likely still in Eden. If he was here, Chad would find him. But why would Lyle avoid him?

Minutes ticked by, minutes Chad could ill afford to lose without casting suspicion on his whereabouts. Knowing his prey had escaped him for now, knowing time was short, Chad had sprinted back to Brittany, figuring he'd been gone ten minutes at most. He'd taken another sixty seconds to prepare an alibi and then had strode boldly into the ballroom to find her speaking to a man in a devil's costume.

Glad that security hadn't been called and that Brittany willingly came outside to hear his explanation, Chad led her to a bench on a stone patio where they could look out over the gardens. The cool night air wrapped around Brittany and him, weaving them in a private cocoon that simmered with tension. A nearby fountain spouted water, the trickling murmur soothing against the background music from the party, now at a low enough volume for them to talk over.

"Sorry I had to depart so abruptly," Chad began.

Her tone was tight with tension. "You weren't in the rest room."

"I went there first, hoping the attendant might have safety pins or a needle and thread. When he didn't have what I needed, I returned to the dressing rooms," he lied. "My pants split down the seam."

"You could have told me."

"I didn't want to risk exposing myself in the middle of the dance floor."

Her gaze dropped and he twisted around to show her the side seam he'd torn and then pinned to confirm his alibi. He chuckled easily, deliberately making her uncomfortable, hoping she'd drop the questions. "I didn't wear anything underneath."

She sucked in her breath, the pinched look leaving her mouth. "You came in through the front. The side entrance is closest to the dressing rooms."

"But I knew you'd be looking for me near the men's room. And I appreciate your concern, but..." He hesitated, hoping to provoke her question, leading her where he wanted her to go.

"But what?"

Bingo! She fell quite nicely into his little trap. A trap where he could turn the tables, lead her away from the subject he didn't want to discuss and put her on the defensive. "Are you always this possessive?"

She crossed her arms over her chest, her chin lifted in defiance. "I thought you might be sick. I'm not possessive."

"Okay." He dropped the matter, but let her know he didn't believe her by his teasing tone. Testing to see if she'd allow his touch, he put an arm over her shoulder and drew her against his side. She didn't relax, but she didn't struggle, either, and he figured he'd negotiated a temporary truce. "Would you like to go back inside?"

"Parties really aren't my thing."

"I assume we don't have the Ravishment Room reserved in your name a little later," he teased, not even waiting for a negative response before he continued. "So what would you like to do?"

She stood, stiffly. "Why don't we call it a night? I'm beat."

Her shoulders sagged with a touch of weariness, and even in the moonlight, he imagined he saw shadows under her eyes. So her next words surprised him. "Would you mind if we walked?"

He held out his arm, wondering if she'd take it. "Your wish is my command. But won't you get cold in that harem outfit?"

She hesitated, without taking his arm. "Mom's house is about a mile or so up the road. Let's change out of these costumes and meet back here in a few minutes."

Chad agreed, found the men's area and changed

from his costume with speed. He wanted to be waiting for her when she arrived. Although he'd known his absence would cause some suspicion, and although she'd seemed to buy his story, the warmth and beginnings of trust he'd worked so hard to create earlier had vanished. She'd allowed him to put his arm over her shoulder, but it was if their kiss, their dance, their teasing had never happened. Brittany may have accepted his explanation on the surface, but deep down, she didn't trust him.

Some man must have done a real number on her. Chad knew he would have to be more careful in the future. It would take time and patience to repair the damage he'd done tonight. Still, as he tucked his shirt into his jeans and slipped on his shoes, he felt more than up to the challenge.

FEW CARS PLIED the roads since Eden's residents preferred to use golf carts. Chad and Brittany strolled the gentle hills in silence, taking in the estates that were built on huge tracts of land, each one protected by massive front gates and sophisticated security systems. Dense forests of pine and oak maintained the owners' privacy and prevented Chad from seeing the buildings beyond the long, winding driveways.

Chad didn't press Brittany into conversation, fearing he might inadvertently push another hot button. Since his things had been moved to the Barrington residence, Brittany hadn't canceled his contract, and he would be satisfied with that—for now.

In the moonlight, he spied deer, possums, a raccoon

and several horses grazing in well-tended pastures. For long stretches of pavement, there was little to see beyond the forest and its wildlife.

After about thirty minutes of steady walking, Brittany pointed to a set of gates. "Home sweet home."

They entered the property after Brittany pressed a security code which Chad carefully memorized. Then they walked through the gate and around a bend, their slow pace giving him time to notice the security cameras' locations and peruse the alarm system on the surprisingly modest A-frame made of cedar and glass. He'd expected a mansion, not a cozy dwelling that melded with the parklike setting, surrounded by a buffer zone of flowering rosebushes.

A complete circuit around the perimeter would have to wait till morning. For now he needed to settle into his new quarters without casting any additional suspicions on himself or his reason for being there.

As they walked up to the door, automatic lights came on. Brittany took out a key and he unlocked the door. Up close he could see beyond the expert makeup job to the circles beneath her hazel eyes. They were a lovely shade of hazel, a cross between the grandiose Mississippi and a classified Pacific atoll about a thousand miles due south southwest of Hawaii.

"Come on in." Her voice was cool, yet he heard the trace of a tremor beneath the polite words, a tremor he longed to goad until she lost her polished veneer.

While he would have liked to take her into his arms

for another kiss, would have enjoyed replacing the uncertainty hovering in her eyes with something more pleasant, he had to keep his job in mind. He had to remember he was a highly paid man-of-the-month and he couldn't afford to antagonize her further.

Up close, Brittany's unforgettable eyes took him in with a blend of quiet curiosity and blatant wariness. Yet her frosty expression couldn't hide the promise of the warmth underneath. Despite her determined efforts to do so.

"You sure you want me here?" Chad asked, refusing to step over the threshold.

At his question, one haughty eyebrow raised, but not before he caught a glimpse of hurt and maybe a tad of anger. "You wouldn't be here if I didn't want you."

He wouldn't touch that line even if he had an AK-47 assault rifle to defend himself. Brittany's voice had remained cool, composed, yet Chad was an especially perceptive man. His sisters had taught him that women didn't always say what they meant or react in accordance with how they felt. SEAL training had taught him to be wary of people who acted one way when they clearly thought differently. Combat training had taught him to look beneath the surface for the meaning behind the outward appearance.

Brittany was one alluring bundle of seductive contradictions. She kissed like his hottest fantasy and wore her provocative clothing, tight black capri pants and a snug white tank top, like a suit of armor. The arrogant tilt of her head, the set of her jaw and her compressed lips told him she wanted him to think she didn't welcome him here. Yet nothing could disguise the interested gleam in her eyes as, despite herself, she leaned toward him, close enough for him to recall her scent and the taste of her kiss and how good she had felt in his arms.

He forced his thoughts to business. "What's on the agenda for tomorrow?"

"I thought we'd hang out."

Those words from another woman's lips might have been a tempting invitation. He suspected Brittany wanted to avoid him. The house might not be large, but if they didn't go out in public, she wouldn't have to play half of a couple.

She gestured downward, to casement windows that in daytime would let light into an underground room. "There's an exercise area and a heated swimming pool in the basement. We have satellite television, too, so you shouldn't be bored."

"What about you?" he asked, wondering what she was up to. For the first time, she almost seemed to relax, as if she thought she could share a house with him and forget the kiss they'd shared. She might be able to fool herself. He knew better.

Brittany gestured for him to come inside. "I'm not going anywhere."

Chad entered a living room with tongue-and-groove oak flooring, contemporary art hanging over the massive stone fireplace and comfy-looking leather couches. The decor didn't interest him, not when he had such an enticing view of Brittany's back. He suspected he might become very familiar with that part of her anatomy since she kept walking away from him. He didn't mind. She had a graceful neckline, strong, squared shoulders that tapered to a petite waist, very rounded hips and…she spun around to catch him staring at her butt.

"I was admiring the decor."

She crossed her arms over her chest. "The house is my mother's, but she's staying at the spa to give us some privacy."

"So we're all alone?"

She nodded. "Knowing mother, I'm sure she'll be stopping by to check on us."

He strode over to the fireplace, giving her plenty of room—room enough so she wouldn't feel threatened. "Aren't you a little old for—?"

"My mother and I made a deal. She's making sure I uphold my end."

"No wonder you're so reluctant." He suddenly understood some of her contradictions. "You don't like the bargain, do you?"

Her lips tightened. "I agreed to her terms."

"You mind telling me what they are?"

"It's not your concern."

"I think it is." He closed the distance in the blink of an eye, stopping inches from her until they stood toe to toe. He'd known his quick advance would be threatening, but he wanted her the slightest bit off balance. Upsetting her brought out the boldness and courage he admired so much.

He had to give her credit. She didn't step back. She

didn't retreat. Her hazel eyes darkened as her pupils widened.

She tilted her head back slightly to look him in the eye and he found her courage exciting. Especially when her brazen look contrasted with the pulse racing at her neck. "All you need to know is that I agreed to spend a month in Eden."

"With me?"

"With a man."

He let his tone soften to a husky whisper. "So any man would do?"

She spun on her heel and twisted away from him. "Damn you. This isn't easy for me."

It was odd that she made such admissions under pressure, but that was when her boldness and honestly came out. His first instinct was to trap her until she told him the exact nature of the bargain she'd made, until she admitted that she liked his arms around her, that she liked kissing him, but she sounded so defenseless, he thought that she was too vulnerable to have this conversation right now. So he put his questions on the back burner and changed the subject.

"So where's our bedroom?"

CHAD'S CHARM HADN'T dissuaded Brittany from showing him a guest bedroom where she'd left him for the night. With a full bath, a king-size bed and a view of the mountains, she figured he should have a comfortable night. Since Eden's efficient staff had delivered his belongings during the masquerade ball, Chad was all set to settle in.

Unfortunately, upstairs in her room that had been decorated in soft turquoises and golds, she felt as shaky as a tightrope walker in a strong wind without a safety net. One moment she felt her old self—confident, bold, balanced—but when the slightest breeze upset her equilibrium, she overreacted and lost both her confidence and stability.

Case in point: Chad's ten-minute vanishing act to repair a split seam in his costume. Before her marriage to Devlin, she wouldn't have been bothered if a date had left her alone for so short a time period. Before coming to Eden, she'd thought she'd healed and returned to her former self, but apparently she wasn't there yet. After her overreaction tonight, she realized that not only did she have trust issues with the opposite sex, she could no longer trust her own reactions. If she didn't sort out and fix the problem, she could end up one of those neurotic women who required her man to account for every minute of his day.

Just because Devlin had cheated on her didn't mean all men were untrustworthy. Just because he'd hurt her didn't mean she now had to react out of fear of betrayal with every new man she met. Only how did she regain her ability to trust? How did she repair the damage?

If she had suspected Devlin's duplicity during their marriage, the shocking ending wouldn't have devastated her so. She had seen exactly what she'd wanted to see. She'd thought Devlin perfect. She'd thought their marriage perfect. She'd been so unprepared for reality that she still couldn't trust her own judgment. Then his string of affairs made tabloid news and printed her failure for the world to see. Damn him. She thought she was over her past, but she'd merely hidden. In Eden she could no longer hide—not from her past, not from Chad, not from herself.

Brittany had changed into a baggy T-shirt and cotton sweatpants. She snapped off her light and flung herself on her bed, knowing she wouldn't sleep for hours. She hated to admit it, but her mother might have been right to bring her here. Within Eden, Brittany should be able to let down her guard, get over her past, move on with her life. In theory, that sounded fine, but Brittany feared the process would elude her.

What the hell was she going to do with Chad Hunter?

WHEN THE DAWN'S FIRST LIGHT broke through her window, Brittany still didn't have a clue. Tired of tossing and turning, she went downstairs to fix herself coffee and heard a heavy-sounding thud in the basement. Chad was also awake and from the sounds echoing up the stairs, he was putting the exercise room to good use.

She fixed two mugs of coffee and wandered downstairs. A fanatic about exercise, Samantha had a room devoted to working off the calories. In addition to a treadmill, weight-lifting equipment and a stair stepper, Samantha had installed a sauna in one corner, a steam bath in another and the heated pool in a connecting room possessing the latest in technology, so the user could swim against a current while remaining in one place.

Barefoot, Brittany walked quietly through the open door to the exercise room, surprised to find Chad had pushed all the equipment along one wall, which left an open area in the rest of the room. Disregarding the expensive equipment, Chad exercised alone, his back to the mirrored front wall. He wore loose white pants, tied at the waist, no shirt and a red band around his forehead. His chest glistened with sweat as he sinuously moved like some kind of kung fu fighter against an invented foe.

Chad dominated the space around him, making it his by his sheer presence. Instrumental music played in the background, and he flexed one glorious muscle after another in a primitive rhythm that held Brittany captivated.

She stared at all those rippling and glistening muscles and forgot about the coffee mugs, forgot that those powerful arms had held her last night. She even had to remind herself to breathe.

He turned toward her, bowed his head, his gaze never leaving her face, never stopping his fluid motion. He began to move faster, seductively, sensuously, like a thread being pulled from a silk cocoon. Brittany recognized Chad was performing some kind of martial arts drill against an imaginary opponent. Using strikes with elbows and kicks, blocks with forearms and shifting maneuvers, he made each move precise, powerful and poetic.

Mesmerized by his blur of actions combined with the grace and power between his gestures, she suspected he was exhibiting the control of a master. And she owned all that power for a month. All she had to do was say the word and…she couldn't go there. Not while her hands trembled and her mouth went dry. Not when she hadn't had a night's sleep and her thoughts burned like fine brandy on a parched throat.

Brittany clamped her teeth together, closed her fingers around the hot mugs, letting the heat bring reality in. She didn't want a man who could cause her to lose a night's sleep after one sizzling kiss followed by a ten-minute disappearance. She didn't want a man who made her lose her appetite. She didn't want a man who made her forget to draw a breath. She didn't want Chad Hunter.

Brittany knew she should turn around and leave, but resigned herself to enjoy the show. She'd seen him wearing a skimpy vest, knew he had a powerful chest. It was undeniably sexy seeing his muscles in action, inordinately seductive watching his concentration, quietly sensual the way every smooth action lacked any inefficient movement. She couldn't help appreciating the smooth flexion and extension of bronze flesh, couldn't force herself to miss one minute of his spectacular performance.

He ended in a flurry of hand movements while his lower torso remained still, his powerful thighs rooting his legs into the wooden floor. As if honoring an opponent, he straightened, brought his feet together, and let his arms drop against his sides. He bowed, then straightened, his gaze locking with Brittany's. "Good morning."

Heat flooded her cheeks. Her skipping heart danced into her throat as if she was a voyeur unable to pull her gaze away from that magnificent body, yet also unable to maintain the eye contact she found so unnerving.

Dropping her gaze to the coffee mugs, she offered him one. "Hope you like it black."

"Thanks." He accepted the cup, eyeing her over the brim as he sipped. "Didn't you sleep?"

Damn, he was observant. Without Samantha to nag her, Brittany had forgotten to apply makeup to hide the dark circles under her eyes that revealed her sleepless night. Besides, she'd hardly expected her houseguest to be up at the crack of dawn.

She shrugged and kept her words vague, hoping he wouldn't press for details. "I had things on my mind."

"That's one of the reasons I exercise. Focused concentration is a great release of tension." He set down his coffee mug. "Care to join me?"

"I don't...I—"

"I won't hurt you."

She eyed him up and down from the corded muscles in his neck to his taut and lean stomach. She'd bet he even had muscles in his toes. "You probably don't know your own strength."

"Chicken." His tone was light, but his eyes dared her with a gleam that prodded her to accept his challenge.

She resisted. "I'm being prudent."

"If I taught you some moves, you would know where and how to hurt a guy. The skills might come in handy one day. Besides..." he hesitated.

"What?"

"Since you aren't into pleasure, you might as well get something for your mother's money. I'm expensive."

In more ways than one. He might have cost her mother a bundle, but Brittany was the one who'd lost untold hours of sleep. Still, they had to spend their time doing something.

She set down her coffee mug next to his. "You know what rich people say about living on a budget?"

"What?"

"A budget is an attempt to live below your yearnings."

He gestured for her to join him on some floor mats. "And what do you yearn for?"

She grinned. "Right now, I'd settle for a technique that would throw you across the room."

7
_____

BRITTANY'S WORDS might have sounded tough
enough, but as she followed Chad to the mats, she
wondered if she was making a mistake. He towel-
dried the sweat off his face, arms and chest, and she
tried not to think what kind of havoc his kind of
power could wreak. She'd seen the man punch and
kick at speeds fast enough to blur, speeds her eyes
couldn't even follow. She really had no business putting herself into so vulnerable a position....

Yet, because he did have such control over every
precise cock of his wrist and kick of his feet, she
figured he wouldn't make a mistake and hurt her by
accident.

"The first and most important thing you must remember," Chad told her, his tone serious as he tossed
the towel aside, "is that you aren't allowed to hurt
the instructor."

At the absurdity of his words, she laughed. Unless
she accidentally struck an unprotected area, she didn't
think even her best shot could put a dent in him. He
sat on the mat and gestured for her to do the same,
but she didn't see any weak spots. He looked like he
had muscles on his muscles, yet his quiet confidence

assured her, despite that he probably outweighed her by close to a hundred pounds.

Even the position he took as he sat on the mats was precise, his back straight, legs spread. "Let's stretch a little first."

She followed his lead without much difficulty, the stretching exercises similar to the ones she used to warm up before playing tennis. Her stomach rolled nervously, reminding her this was no civilized tennis match where the opponents never made physical contact except for a handshake over the net at the game's completion. Chad's sport was full contact.

"Besides throwing your instructor across the room, is there anything else you want me to teach you?" Chad asked as he grabbed the backs of his calves and pulled his torso down to his knee.

Again she copied his moves. "What are the choices?"

"Karate, jujitsu, hand-to-hand or self-defense?"

She should have known he was a man who took his fighting as seriously as he'd taken to teasing her. "Which one produces the least amount of bruises?"

He raised a brow and stretched out his chest over his other leg. "I told you, no bruising the instructor."

"It's not *your* body I'm worried about."

He winked at her. "It's my job to worry about yours."

Yesterday, if he'd made that remark, she would have wanted to slap him. Today she'd learned to take his teasing in the same spirit as he dished it out.

While she tried to ignore how his words so often

carried double entendres, she stretched her hamstrings, feeling her leg muscles slowly loosen. "Then I'll leave the decision of what we do today up to you."

He turned his head and his sky-blue eyes locked with hers. "I decide what we do—*all* day?"

She hadn't said that. He was putting words in her mouth. Yet the intriguing blue flames in his eyes were so irresistible that, instead of automatically protesting, she thought twice. She didn't want to get burned, but this was Eden. She had the final say. Why not let him plan their day? She certainly had put no thought into how they would spend their time, except to get through it with as little emotional turbulence as possible.

Besides it might be interesting to see what he came up with. She'd already set the limits on the relationship. Why not put herself into his so very capable hands? She was thinking figuratively, of course, and realized now he had her finding double entendres in every phrase, too.

"Fine. You be social director for the day," she agreed, hoping he didn't realize that she hadn't given another person that much control over her in years.

"Self-defense is where we'll start then." He stood and she shoved to her feet, wondering what she was in for.

"Have you ever hit anyone?" he asked.

"Only in my nightmares."

"Okay. What you need to remember then is that precision counts more than force. If you're ever attacked, the most important thing is to keep your wits about you. Since it takes years to develop the skills of an expert, we'll concentrate on strikes that take more thought than sheer power or proficient timing.''

As he spoke, she slowly relaxed. Chad wasn't going to attack her. Nor was he going to use his superior skills to put her in body holds that would make her uncomfortable. A complete and thorough professional, he seemed intent on actually teaching her how to defend herself.

Within thirty minutes, she became so engrossed in his instructions she forgot her initial hesitancy. He showed her what to do if someone put a gun to her head—distract her attacker, shove the weapon away from her body and twist the wrist until her foe dropped the gun. He showed her what to do if a mugger grabbed her from behind and put his arm around her throat—stomp his foot, ram her elbow into his gut, duck and swivel free.

Never once did he make her feel awkward by showing off his own skill. Never once did he tease her over her lack of strength. Instead, he seemed intent on teaching her how to maximize her advantage against a bigger and stronger opponent. Each time, he demonstrated the movements precisely, helping until she understood how to duplicate his techniques. And her respect for him grew.

''The trick is remembering which skill to use because a victim is almost always taken by surprise,'' he told her.

After an hour, her body was warm but not overly

sore. A light sweat had broken out over her flesh, and she was breathing a tad raggedly, but he'd paced the workout so she felt good, not exhausted.

"There's one more technique I'd like to show you, but it can wait for another day."

"I'm not that tired."

"Okay." He stretched out on the mat on his back with his hands up by his head. "Pretend I'm you. You're in bed." She'd rather not think about bed. "You've been sleeping and you wake up to find a man holding you down."

"What do I do?"

"Straddle my hips," he told her. "And press down on my wrists with your hands."

She did as he instructed, doing her best to ignore the intimacy of her splayed thighs around his waist, her breasts close to his face as she held down his wrists.

"Now I'm going to pretend that you're too strong for me to dislodge by using my hands."

"If our positions were reversed, there is no way I could get free."

"You can if you employ leverage," he instructed. "Turn your head and watch my legs."

She did as he asked and saw him pull both legs to one side until he twisted around, his body forming an L shape. Then he cocked one knee, flattening his foot on the ground to push, and used a twisting motion of the hips to roll her off him.

"Your turn."

Eager to see if the technique would work but a little

uneasy about letting him place her in such a submissive and helpless position, she did as he instructed. Suddenly she realized that during the past hour, she'd learned much more than self-defense. She trusted Chad. He'd been so gentle, the only soreness she might feel later would be from overworked sinews and tendons.

Not once had he touched, brushed against her or grabbed her inappropriately, not even accidentally. He'd been a perfect gentleman.

So she didn't hesitate to lie on her back and allow him to hold down her wrists. "Should I scream?"

He shook his head. "Save it for when you thrust me off with your hips. It'll give you more energy at the right time."

She twisted her legs to one side, but she couldn't roll him off.

"Don't try to dislodge my hand on your wrist but pull your hand down toward your legs," he instructed.

And suddenly she got it. With her legs twisted sideways and with one hand still held by him but now closer to her waist than her head, she could buck her hips to roll him off. She climbed to her feet easily. "That's a pretty good trick, but if you weighed much more, I don't think it would work."

"No one technique works against every opponent. You did great."

His compliment warmed her. His instructions had been a fine way to start the day. She wouldn't mind working out with him again.

"Let's cool down with a few stretches."

As her body slowly cooled down while they worked through another series of stretching exercises, she realized that Chad had established a camaraderie between them that she hadn't shared with a man for a long time. At her charity foundation, she worked with men, but they were employees, not friends. Being with Chad was different because he'd taken the time to establish a personal trust.

After stretching, she picked up a towel and headed for the combination steam bath and shower. "I won't be long. You can use the sauna while you wait for me."

She stepped into the changing room and kicked off her sweatpants. Still in her T-shirt, she started a little at a knock on the door. Wrapping a towel around her waist, she opened it.

"How do you feel about a massage before your shower?" Chad asked her with a grin.

"Excuse me?"

"I studied massage and you're going to be sore. I can make you feel better."

She stared into his eyes, wondering what he was up to. Seeing only honest intentions, she slowly and hesitantly nodded. She supposed her acceptance was a measure of the trust he'd established between them. For once, she didn't want to analyze her motives. She always enjoyed a massage, knew she would be sore and his hands would feel good on her. "Where do you want me?"

He grabbed four, clean rolled-up towels that were

stacked and ready for use outside the steam bath. "Over here."

Chad gestured to the mats. He spread out one towel for her to lie upon and held the others aside as she positioned herself facedown on the mat.

"What's with the extra towels?" she asked.

"Lift your hips."

She did as he requested and he slipped two of the rolled towels under her.

"Now bend your knees."

She did and he placed the last roll on the floor so that when she lowered her limbs, her legs remained slightly bent.

"Comfy?"

"So comfortable I might fall asleep."

"Lying straight and stiff isn't a natural way for the body to relax."

"This is much better."

"And it'll ease the tightness of your lower back."

She hadn't noticed she was getting sore there until he mentioned the spot. Chad Hunter was damn observant. Either that or he knew from experience where the exercises they'd done strained the body.

She expected him to straddle her back, but he knelt beside her. "There's one more thing."

"What?"

"I work better on skin."

His words rang an alarm bell somewhere in her mind, but she was so relaxed and was so much anticipating those clever hands on her that she didn't immediately refuse. "What are you proposing?"

She felt his hands on the towel by her waist at the edge of her T-shirt. "Let me pull this over your head. The material can pillow your head."

He gave her a second to object. When she remained silent and lifted up slightly to help him, he lifted her shirt over her head and placed the cotton between her cheek and the towel. He didn't totally free her arms, though, which remained bent and relaxed by her head, tangled in the shirt. But if she moved, she'd expose her breasts because she hadn't taken time to don a bra before she'd padded downstairs for her morning coffee. However, if she held still, she retained her modesty.

She was by no means tied up, but partially restrained, only her back bared to him, the towel still snug about her waist. She could have put a halt to the proceedings, but she couldn't help anticipating what he would do next. The man was full of surprises, and if this was his idea of a seduction, she'd receive a mighty good rubdown before she finally told him no.

Still, he might be positioning her just for a massage. She'd had several massages at various spas that Samantha had dragged her to. Always she'd first removed her clothes and simply lain beneath a bath towel or sheet. However Chad was not a professional masseur. Still, the past hour had taught her to trust him with her body.

She turned her head to look at him and reassure herself, but the light in his blue eyes didn't give her a clue to his thoughts. "You happy now?"

"I'm getting there." He stepped away from her. "I

need some cocoa butter. Stay there and I'll be right back.''

He walked out of the room without a glance back. Though she should probably yank her shirt down, climb to her feet and take a shower, then a long nap, it seemed too much of an effort. It also seemed too much effort to work up any anger toward Chad for making her so comfortable, lifting her shirt and then abandoning her before he'd even touched her.

Her muscles went limp as overcooked noodles. The lack of sleep and the strenuous exercise had caught up with her, taking the edge off her normal wariness. Lying on the mat, waiting for him to return while her mind conjured images of his hands on her back was simply too good a fantasy to interrupt.

Cool air on her bare skin, her hands twisted in her shirt, her hips propped at an angle, she waited. Waited for him to return while she wondered exactly what kind of massage he had in mind and how far he would go. How far she wanted him to go.

Anticipation flowed through her. She was missing his presence and aching for his attention—and he had yet to offer the slightest touch.

The man knew how to set a scene. If, a week ago, someone had told her that she'd be lying on the floor, her breath hitching in anticipation as she waited for a man to come to her, she'd have laughed in denial, positive she would never be in this predicament.

And while she told herself that she might be opening herself up for disillusionment, she didn't expect Chad to love her like a husband. Like she'd expected

Devlin to love her. Eden wasn't the real world. Eden was a safe haven where she could let Chad wash away the layers of distrust that had coated her every thought since her divorce. Her time in Eden could be a time of renewal. If she let it.

What could be taking Chad so long?

A minute or two later he walked through the door with a jar of cocoa butter in his hand, and she knew what had kept him. With his dark hair slicked back and water droplets spiking his eyelashes, it was apparent he'd taken time for a quick shower. Still shirtless but minus the workout pants, he'd slipped on a pair of shorts that allowed her to appreciate the hewn musculature in his calves, dusted with a light covering of dark hair. All too aware of him, she could smell his spicy sandalwood soap and had to fight a sharp spike of impatient desire.

"I almost fell asleep," she lied, not wanting him to know that the tasty sight and savory scent of him were creating a craving for his touch that was way out of proportion to the anticipation of a simple massage. Obviously, part of her was thinking about his hands on her far differently than how she would a massage from a professional. It had been so long since a man had touched her that if she wasn't careful, she would overreact.

Again she thought he would come to her. Again he left her waiting while he picked out a CD. The mellow tones of Pink Floyd brought her back to a happier time when Brittany had been in college and still believed in fairy tales and happy endings. She wondered if she would have liked Chad if she had met him then.

Probably. He was charming, knew how to tease her into a good mood, and he was serious about his work. And right now he was about to focus all that marvelous energy on her.

Finally he approached, and she distracted herself from her edginess by talking. "How'd you end up in the navy?"

Unscrewing the jar, he knelt beside her. The scent of cocoa butter wafted to her, and she wondered if she'd ever smell that erotic scent again without thinking of his long fingers dipping into the cream. She inhaled deeply, letting the tropical coconut fragrance lead her down a path she'd never been, accepting that she wanted more than the emptiness of the past few years, wanted more than a satisfying job, wanted more than she'd allowed herself in a long, long while.

Having no idea of the thoughts her mind had taken, he answered the question she'd asked. "In high school, I joined a swim team and realized I had some talent. An athletic scholarship paid my way through college, which helped out a lot at home. With seven kids, my folks couldn't afford to pay for all that higher education."

"I don't know how large families can afford kids."

"Between odd jobs, scholarships, grants and loans, we all finished college." He lifted her hair away from her neck and a shiver of expectation trembled down her spine. "You cold?"

"I'm fine." The flesh at the back of her nape tingled, eager for more of his touch. "After college you joined the navy?"

He straddled her hips and smoothed the cocoa butter onto his hands, then spread the warmed lubricant over her back in broad, uniform strokes of spiraling heat. His hands were large, strong, and knew where to spend an extra moment to soothe.

"Mmm. That feels great."

Using his palms, the heel of his hands and his long fingers, he worked her tendons, covering every part of her back, leaving no inch of flesh untended.

"I joined the navy, saw the world. Got married and divorced," he said the words lightly, his fingers digging out the knots in her shoulders and applying pressure to the muscles.

"Why did you split up?" His marriage hadn't ended because the man was bad with his hands. His clever fingers seemed to know exactly where she was tight and had the knack of rubbing the cramped muscles until she melted like wax under a flame.

"I was never home."

"Why not?" Had he cheated on his wife, too? For a moment she wanted to swat away his hands, but forced herself not to jump to conclusions. Not every man cheated on his wife. She listened carefully to his answer, knowing it mattered a great deal to her what he said next.

"I had another mistress." She stiffened, holding her breath. "The navy took all my time." His hands found the stiffness, and he employed his thumbs to erase her tension, continuing to speak only after she released her breath. "My wife needed more attention than I gave her. So we split up and went our separate ways."

"You make it sound so painless."

"We were kids. The marriage only lasted six months. I was gone for most of them. I don't blame her for finding someone else."

"You're very...forgiving."

His fingers skimmed down her spine, working out the soreness of her lower back. "Tender here?"

"How do you know?"

His thumbs caressed her lower back, circling under the towel, loosening the terry cloth while he kneaded until her bottom lay exposed, except for a sliver of towel down her center. "Your gluteus maximus muscles are tight, right here."

His fingers applied pressure to the knotted muscles of her buttocks. He scooted down her legs and the towel dropped away.

She sucked in a gasp. Now was the time to stop him. She clenched her knees together realizing that with her hips propped up, her thighs were parted slightly as if she was asking for more of his attentions.

Before she could think, before she decided what she wanted, his warm hands were back, caressing her bare bottom, his knuckles gently working against a soreness she hadn't known existed. Creating a heat she didn't know how to cool. She was no longer thinking about tight muscles and knots. Instead, her pulse racheted up several notches. Her mouth went dry as every repressed sexual feeling that she'd held back over the past few years came at her full speed.

She'd thought her sex life had been more than adequate during her marriage, but if Chad's experienced hands were any indication of what she'd been missing, then she'd misjudged Devlin badly. Making love to Devlin had been about pleasing *him*. Somehow, she'd never felt quite up to the task. With Chad, she didn't need to twitch one sore muscle to feel feminine. She already felt warm enough for steam to sizzle off her flesh.

Still she managed a feeble protest that sounded needy even to her own ears. "What are you doing?"

"Whatever feels good." His hands lightly moved in soft circles over her bottom. "Do you like this?"

She bit back a plea for more. "I don't—"

"How about this?" He lightly caressed the insides of her thighs, and she fought back a moan rising in the back of her throat at the powerful sensations pooling between her thighs. She was suddenly so close to an orgasm that if she clamped her thighs together, she could—

He placed one knee between hers, as if he knew exactly how ready she was, knew exactly what she wanted.

But he was keeping her there balanced on the brink between stepping over the edge and flying away, and the sensations had her ready to beg. Never had she been so ready. Never had need risen up so quickly. Never had she fought so hard she could think of nothing else but the super-slow tease of his fingers and where she wanted them to go next. Her fists clenched the T-shirt. She waited, barely able to keep her hips from rising up to meet him.

He had yet to offer her the most intimate of caresses. Instead, he tempted her flesh with silky, smooth circles that teased, taunted, tantalized. "Samantha implied that you're divorced, too?"

"Yes." Was she answering his question or responding to his hands and urging him on? She no longer knew.

"What happened?"

"He…cheated. And with a woman—not a job." Her voice was hoarse and husky with need.

His fingers slipped to the insides of her thighs and she wondered if it was possible to fly apart even before he touched her intimately. She could barely hear his words through the spell of desire he'd woven around her like a magician.

"His cheating came as a surprise?"

She gritted her teeth and told herself not to move, not to part her legs wider. Although every cell in her body urged her to do so, it was possible Chad had no idea how much he was turning her on. "I thought our marriage was perfect. I thought I could make him happy."

"He did the cheating and you blamed yourself?"

The pain of her failure still stabbed her, but the sharp agony had been replaced by another kind of ache. His fingers lightly stroked up and down the insides of her knees and her thighs, and the craving that had so gently simmered, now boiled and flared into a white-hot flame of need.

She gasped as his fingers moved away from the fire he'd started. Suddenly she realized he could be offering what she wanted. All she had to do was ask.

# 8

THROUGH THE DRAWN BLINDS, the basement's casement windows cast riveting shadows and intriguing light over Brittany's skin, skin now bared to Chad's touch, quivering beneath the pads of his fingertips. Pliant and soft as fine suede, warm as rich caramel, her flesh, so sensitive to his lightest caress, was a silky texture he would never forget.

He let his fingers linger on the insides of her tender thighs, drawing tidy, tempting circles. Slowly she thawed from icy hard to a wonderfully warm woman riding the razor's edge of desire. Eventually he would give her more, but first he would see exactly how far she would let him go.

He enjoyed taking complete control, enjoyed the power he wielded as she responded to him—no doubt against her will. His ice princess wanted to pretend she didn't have needs and that she didn't want him, which made her trembling all the sweeter. She wanted him to continue, and even if she wouldn't speak the words, her body was plainly talking to him.

Her breathing was no longer even. Muscles he'd worked hard to relax quivered with lust. A sugary dampness spread between her thighs, and he breathed in her musky essence, pleased by her feminine heat.

Watching her transform, forcing her to come to terms with the passionate woman she'd tried to hide, was causing satisfaction he'd never known to well up in his chest. That he could make her want him, that he had won her trust, unkinked a knot inside him that he'd never known was there.

Since his wife had left him, he'd let women pick him up in bars, knowing they wanted the same thing he did—a night of pleasure and no commitments. Those women had come to him already primed for sex. Making love with Brittany was different. He'd had to work to please her, and that made having her open and eager and ready for him all the more exciting.

In absolutely no hurry, he skimmed his fingers down the inside of her parted legs to her knees, noting with satisfaction that as her hands clenched the T-shirt, her legs parted another millimeter, silently asking him to reverse the direction of his massage.

"I could touch you like this all day," he murmured with husky pleasure as the cocoa butter melted into her golden skin. He traced fingers behind her knees, watched little goose bumps rise up in response. Slowly he caressed her calves, her ankles, her feet.

"I...didn't...know feet could...be so...sensitive."

Her voice, raw with passion yet oddly hesitant, made him go easier on her. He'd been about to ask her to turn over, to delay her ultimate pleasure. He longed to explore her breasts, discover their texture and color and size, ached to know if her nipples were hard with wanting, but he refused to selfishly break the mood.

Taking one of her feet in his hands, he rubbed the instep, appreciating her square toes, the close-clipped nails, the high and delicate arch. "The navy sent me to Japan to learn hand-to-hand combat. While I was there, I learned to appreciate Eastern culture. The Japanese have raised the ritual pleasures of massage to a fine art."

He ran his knuckles along her arches.

"Ooh, that feels good. What else did you learn?"

Her comment was probably as close to begging as she would ever get. Chad teased her a little more. "I mastered the use of chopsticks."

She groaned as he pressed deeper with his knuckles. "What else?"

"I bathed with strangers, Japanese men and women."

"And?"

"Afterward, I always had a massage." He straightened and applied cocoa butter between her toes. "I find a good rubdown rejuvenates the skin and joints."

She giggled. "That tickles."

Her feet weren't all he intended to tickle. He couldn't wait to put his hands on every part of her. Damn, she was a fine-looking woman. On her stomach, legs slightly parted, hips raised from the rolled towels beneath her, she looked lush, primed, ready. His mouth watered at the glimpse of pink, tender flesh peaking out from blond curls.

*Slow and easy.*

He placed her foot back on the mat, parting her legs enough to place both of his knees between hers. She let out a soft whoosh of air from the back of her throat, but not one word of encouragement did she utter. It was as if she wanted to leave everything to him. Clearly she'd decided not to talk about what was happening, because then she'd have to come to grips with her clearly uncharacteristic behavior.

She might be trembling before him, but she was one stubborn lady. He already knew she responded to teasing. Apparently she needed more of a different kind. The kind that would make her forget everything except him. His hand. His mouth.

And suddenly he decided that as much as he ached to dip his fingers into the core of her heat, place his mouth on her and taste her essence, there was something he wanted more. Much more. He wanted to hear her beg. And he wanted to hear her shout his name when she came.

BRITTANY DIDN'T MOVE while Chad continued to tease her with his massage. She was too busy biting her lip, too busy trying to keep from letting loose tiny moans of pleasure. She'd never done anything like this before and couldn't believe she was feeling so hot.

But he took her totally by surprise as he settled his butt between her knees, his thighs spread over her legs, his knees bent so that his calves pressed against the outside of her legs. His weight and legs wrapped over and around hers, trapping her, preventing her from closing her thighs—not that she had any intention of doing that. With her hands somehow having become so twisted in the T-shirt, she really couldn't move at all.

Emotionally frayed, she ached for him so much her stomach clenched and knotted and reknotted with the wanting. Damn the man. Was he going to take all day? Apparently. His fingers caressed up the insides of her thighs, and she almost screamed at him to hurry, almost pounded her fists into the mat with frustration.

She was so open. So ready for him. What was he waiting for?

She was hot enough to singe his fingers if only he'd touch her. She missed being married. Missed making love. Had never wanted a man like she did now.

She couldn't remember Devlin *ever* focusing so much on her. She'd often suspected his foreplay had been only to turn her on enough so she wouldn't refuse his advances. Chad's massage was solely about her. About her feeling good. About her desires. She needn't do anything. In fact, with the way he had her pinned, she couldn't do more than anticipate his next touch.

And the waiting had her trembling until she could no longer think of anything except the next caress of Chad's hands. Of where he would stroke next.

Finally he brushed his fingers over her curls, shooting a lick of fire deep inside. She spoke without thinking, barely cognizant of the husky need in her tone. "Please."

He fingered the fine hair between her legs, tugging gently on heated flesh that demanded to be touched. "Please, what?"

She ground out the word, fought against rocking her hips. "More."

"Like this?" His touch was so light. Teasing. Taunting. Light enough that she burned so hot she forgot she wasn't going to plead with him.

"Touch me," she demanded, knowing that if he didn't give her more right then, right now, she wouldn't be able to hold back a scream of frustration.

He parted her soft folds and cool air only fanned the flames. She needed…she needed…

And then he was there, expertly touching. She trembled, her back arching, her hips lifting, her body gathering itself for release. Just one more caress, one more stroke, and she would be there.

He withdrew his touch, lightly running his fingers over her bottom, leaving her hanging. On the edge between light and dark, hovering on a cloud of need between sweet pain and dark pleasure, she let out a groan.

"Chad, I…can't…take…any more."

"On the contrary—" his tone was husky with sex "—you'll take it all."

She did buck then, trying to move, trying to close her legs. Frantic, she was close, so close to the most heavenly orgasm and he wouldn't let her…

He placed his hands on her bottom, stretching her open, lifting her hips, exposing her.

"Yes. Please, Chad. Touch me."

He leaned forward and placed his mouth on her. His tongue found her center. Hot. Soft and hard. His tongue flicked over her. She screamed, uncaring, finding release so total she came in one giant explosion.

Like a flame that kept expanding, her orgasm ignited her into an uncontrollable firestorm. She could barely gather her wits, stop her limbs from quivering. She finally understood why, feeling the tension build again.

Chad's mouth was still on her. She might have screamed his name, but he hadn't stopped. She was sensitive enough that it was only moments until she exploded again. Her second orgasm might not have been as powerful as the first, but it lasted longer, so long she lost track of what she said. Sensation that rocked her world diminished to one fiery point, where there was only Chad's mouth and lips and tongue burning exquisite flames into her soul.

She gave up all pretense of sanity. She couldn't draw enough air into her lungs. Her hips bucked. She couldn't take anymore. She couldn't.

"I can't." She sobbed the words.

"You can."

Her body had never absorbed so much pleasure so quickly. She couldn't stand his mouth there. She was too hot, too sensitive. Too out of control.

Oh, God! She was going to come again.

Afterward, she lay quivering like a spent rag doll,

without the energy to speak or turn her head or think while he held her tenderly for a while. She had no idea how long it took for her mind to finally regroup. Eventually her breathing and her heart rate slowed, her spinning senses ground to a stop and she found the strength to open her eyes. Chad had covered her with a towel before he'd stepped across the room to run the water of the shower. While he was occupied, she untwisted her T-shirt from her fingers, pulled it back down over her head and rewrapped the towel around her hips.

Many conflicting emotions assaulted her, and she had trouble sorting through them, even recognizing them. Chad's lovemaking had been a mind-blowing experience. Shaky both mentally and physically, she still knew better than to think what they'd shared was just her lack of sex since her divorce. Sure she'd been going without, depriving herself, maybe even punishing herself for her failed marriage. She'd also not anticipated, expected, or even ever known such pleasure was possible. But none of these facts distracted her from the truth that she wouldn't have reacted that way unless she had feelings for Chad, feelings she had tried to deny, feelings she'd locked up so deep inside her she'd forgotten she possessed a key to free them. And Chad hadn't just picked the lock, he'd flat out busted down the door.

She would deal with it. Later. When she could think past the afterglow, when her head was clear of how she'd reacted to him, clear of his scent, clear of the feel of his clever hands.

As Chad approached her, his eyes bold and gleaming with satisfaction, she was very sure of one thing— their relationship had changed. How could it not after sharing such an intimate act?

That she hadn't expected this development made dealing with her feelings all the more difficult. Uncomfortable. Yet, she couldn't deny that she'd enjoyed the most delicious lovemaking of her life. Still unsure whether her feet would hold her, she tilted up her chin to look Chad in the eyes as he approached.

"Thank you. I guess I needed that more than I knew."

He knelt beside her. "It was my pleasure."

She heard the sincerity in his tone, but his attitude confused her. His ministrations certainly hadn't brought him any pleasure, not in a physical sense. "But you didn't…" She raised her hand and then let it flutter downward, at a loss for words.

"I took pleasure in giving you enjoyment."

She didn't know what to say to such an unselfish statement. For a man to feel that way about lovemaking was an unusual concept for her. She'd had some experience with men before Devlin—not a lot, but some. Enough that she thought she'd known sex with Devlin had been good. She'd been, oh, so wrong. Devlin had been ordinary. Chad was different. Unique. Spectacular. He had a confident strength about him that allowed him to be exceptionally gentle and giving. How could she help but adore that trait in a man? How could she help but melt when he touched her?

Before she could say something heartfelt and silly, Chad scooped her into his arms. He held her like a precious Ming vase, yet she felt so secure she didn't bother to place her arms around his neck. Instead, she simply leaned back and enjoyed the feel of his warm chest against her cheek, the powerful and comforting beat of his heart against her ear and the newfound security of knowing that no way would he drop her.

Sure enough, he eased her to her feet beside the shower, leaving one arm draped around her waist for support. "Would you like company?"

Yes. No. She didn't know, hadn't had time to think things through.

So she went with her gut and took his hand in hers. "You're good company."

Without waiting for his response, she released his hand, yanked the T-shirt over her head and dropped the towel to the floor. She stepped under the warm spray of the shower, but left the door open in a blatant invitation for him to join her.

Tilting her head back, closing her eyes, she let the water rush over her face, slick back her hair and sluice down her neck and shoulders. Within moments, she heard the shower door of the glass enclosure shut, felt his male heat as he joined her.

She didn't open her eyes, didn't turn around, waiting for the water to refresh her. The scent of citrus soap—no it was shampoo—wafted to her on a cloud of spray. Then his hands were in her hair, his fingers massaging her scalp as he worked up a lather.

She reached to brace herself against the tile for support, but he coaxed her into leaning against the hard length of him instead. His fingers in her hair caressed in large soapy circles that soothed and stimulated at the same time.

As his hands washed her, she couldn't help envisioning doing the same to him. She'd enjoy running her hands over him, learning the slope of his muscles, the curve of his chest, the definition of his hips. That fantasy could be fulfilled later, when she didn't feel as if her bones had melted, as if her muscles had forgotten how to support her.

"You want to rinse?" he asked.

She spun to face him, tilted her hair back under the spray, but didn't open her eyes, afraid she might lose her courage. "Soap all of me?"

She sensed him reach for the soap, imagined those capable hands working up a lather. Envisioning his tan hands on her white flesh caused a ripple of pleasure to shoot down her spine as she anticipated warm water, sudsy hands and soft, silky caresses.

His voice, close to her ear, was as smooth as dark molasses. "Where should I start?"

"My breasts." Her answer came without hesitation, boldly provocative, as if the past hurt and pain since her marriage had been erased. She arched into his hands, and like metal forged in heat, she grew stronger than ever before. Still vulnerable, but willing to open herself up to a new experience, willing to open herself to Chad, she felt more alive than ever and ready for new possibilities, once again giving herself a chance to live and feel and make love.

He lifted her breasts with lathered hands. Then his mouth closed on her nipple, his hot tongue seeking, exploring and filling her with exquisite tremors that had her threading her hands into his hair and keeping his head—his mouth—close, as he masterfully created the most divine sensations. His tongue flicked over her nipple, his soapy hands flowed over her shoulders, her back, her bottom until she became so accustomed to his hands on her that she no longer wondered where he would touch next, only how long it would take him to get there.

When he moved his mouth to her other breast and slid his slippery hands between her thighs, she was shocked to find herself ready for him again. Between her lack of sleep and what he'd already wrung from her, she didn't think more was possible.

Still she wanted him inside her. She reached for his hip. He blocked her with his arm as if anticipating her reaction.

He spoke without releasing her breast from between his lips. "Today is for you."

"But—"

His teeth gently bit her nipple. "Don't argue."

"But—"

His hands parted her thighs and touched flesh already sensitive from his previous attentions. Her legs trembled and she had to place her arms on his shoulders to keep herself upright. Surely he couldn't mean for her to come again?

And once more he had her trapped as surely as if he'd locked her in handcuffs. With her nipple taut between his teeth, his tongue licking hot flames straight to her core and his fingers deep inside her, she couldn't have escaped even if she'd wanted to.

She didn't think she could possibly respond again. Yet, he seemed to know her own body better than she did. He kept her trapped until she trembled and quivered and burst into a long, leisurely orgasm that sapped the last of her strength.

So spent, she almost fell and he had to gather her against him to keep her from pooling at his feet like a soggy towel. He rinsed her, helped her out of the shower and dried her.

And when he wrapped her in a giant towel, carried her to her bed and tucked her under the covers, she could barely keep her eyes open. She fell asleep almost the moment her head touched the pillow, secure in the knowledge that they could talk later, and he would still be there when she awakened.


"BRITTANY! CHAD! Are you two decent?" Samantha stood in the front hall at the bottom of the staircase, her gaze searching for her daughter as Chad descended alone.

He'd been about to scout out the hospital in search of records for Lyle, now his reconnaissance mission would have to wait. He told himself to be patient and wait for another opportunity to get away unnoticed.

Glad he'd thrown on shorts before carrying Brittany upstairs, Chad kept his voice even as he greeted the woman in whose house he was living. "Hello, Samantha. Brittany's taking a nap."

Samantha looked put together in a cream blouse, plaid skirt and strappy sandals with quirky heels. At his statement about her daughter, one eyebrow cocked upward at a suggestive angle. "A nap? In the middle of the day? She isn't sick, is she?"

"She's fine. Brittany didn't sleep well last night."

After his attempt to reassure her, Samantha broke into a wide grin. "Wore her out, did you?"

"I don't think I care to answer that."

"Good answer. Protective. Gentlemanly. I like that in a man. I hope Brittany appreciates you."

So did Chad. "Would you like to join me for lunch? I was about to make a sandwich," he improvised.

Samantha stepped forward and looped her arm through his. "And you cook, too? That wasn't in your file."

Chad steered her toward the well-stocked kitchen. "There's probably lots about me that didn't make it into my file. For example, did you know my parents had seven kids and that I have six sisters?"

"Really? No wonder your manners are impeccable." He opened the fridge, retrieved an assortment of cheese and cold cuts, and Samantha took a seat at the breakfast bar.

Chad's father had retired from the military, but his mother hadn't given up her cooking, and thanks to her instruction, he could find his way around a kitchen. While he was no gourmet cook, he could flip a mean omelette, pile meats and cheese on a sandwich as neatly as any of his sisters, even bake chocolate cookies from scratch. Most of all, he had wonderful memories of his family, all gathered in the kitchen, chatting and cooking, delicious smells simmering from the oven and kids running underfoot.

His family remained a close one, and his parents often kept grandchildren under their roof. His mom would have adored this kitchen with all the latest appliances and gadgets. Floor-to-ceiling windows overlooked a rose garden. White marble countertops, a one-of-a-kind stained-glass chandelier and two ovens, a walk-in pantry with a full-size freezer would have kept his mom happily cooking for hours.

He drew plates from the cupboards, silverware from a drawer and glasses from a cabinet. "Actually, officer training includes a seminar on manners. The navy doesn't want us to embarrass the service when we mingle with the public." Chad found rye bread in a drawer, mustard and mayonnaise in the fridge's door. "I thought I might have seen an old acquaintance at the mixer the other night. Maybe you know him?"

Samantha frowned and he wondered if his attempt to sound casual had been too forced. Not only did Chad need to search the hospital for Lyle's records, he needed to begin asking questions if he wanted to find the missing SEAL. Who better to ask than Samantha Barrington, one of Eden's founders?

She drummed her perfectly manicured plum-colored nails absently on the counter. Finally she sighed. "What's his name?"

"Lyle Gates." He set her plate in front of her. "Ever heard of him?"

Samantha shrugged, eyeing the food but not helping herself to so much as an olive. "It's hard to keep the names with the faces. Fifty to a hundred new men come through here every month."

Had she been deliberately vague? Or was he reading more into her evasiveness than the conversation warranted? Chad placed the platter before her. "What would you like to drink?"

"Brandy. It's in the den." She swiveled from her stool. "I'll get it."

Chad didn't say a word. If Samantha Barrington wanted to drink brandy before noon, it was none of his business. Although his question about Lyle hadn't produced any useful information, Chad still had other options. He simply needed to figure out the best way to get in and out of the hospital without being noticed.

Samantha returned with a brandy decanter and twirled a half-full glass between her fingers. Chad poured himself a glass of milk, then made a roast beef sandwich and added cheese, pickles, mustard and salt and pepper, and Samantha stared into her drink, not even pretending to eat. Had she been hoping for an opportunity to talk to him? Perhaps that was why she'd frowned when he'd asked about Lyle. He must have taken the conversation away from where she wanted it to go.

Guessing that Samantha wanted to speak about Brittany wasn't difficult, but he chose to let her bring up whatever was bothering her in her own way.

"You're lucky to have a large family. Brittany and I only have each other." Samantha sighed. "She never knew her father. He died in a motorcycle crash before she was born."

"That must have been tough on you."

"It was tough on both of us." Samantha looked at him, and he saw a deep, painful wound there she did nothing to hide, one he suspected might never heal. She still used her first husband's name and had never remarried, although it had been thirty years. Instead she'd been a single mother to Brittany and built a cosmetic empire. She played with her glass, thoughtful. "Growing up without a father made Brittany different. As a child, she never bonded with a male authority figure. She always liked men and tended to flirt too much as a teenager."

"Brittany?"

"Marriage and divorce changed her." Samantha fiddled with her glass as if debating how much to tell him. "She's been hurt."

"I know."

"I don't want to see her hurt again."

"No parent wants that for their child." Chad recalled one of his sisters crying in his father's arms after a boyfriend had dumped her for her best friend. Two weeks later, his sister had recovered, going to the prom with one of Chad's buddies. His sister had cried only a few tears, but his father had moped around the house for weeks, worried about his daughter. Although his sisters now were all happily married, Dad still worried and so did his mother, although she hid her feelings better. Chad supposed it was the nature of being a parent.

Samantha swirled the brandy in her glass then drilled him with a stare that could have frozen mountains. "I want to be very clear here."

"Shoot." The socialite model was gone. The woman who faced him reminded him of a lioness defending her cub.

"You hurt my daughter and I'll hurt you. Don't underestimate me, Chad. The secretary of the navy is a good friend of mine. Unless you want to be stationed at the North Pole for the rest of your career, you remember what I said."

Well, well. The lioness had claws and wasn't afraid to use them. "Ma'am, are you threatening me?"

Samantha downed the last of her brandy. "I don't make threats. That was a promise. I'm not sure what your agenda is, but I'm warning you. Don't give me a reason to regret choosing you for my daughter."

# 9

BRITTANY WOKE UP from her nap and stretched, feeling deliciously relaxed. A glance at her watch told her it was late afternoon and she'd slept for almost four hours. Refreshed from sleep but not so eager to see Chad right away, she dawdled, brushing her teeth and her hair and dressing, facing the inevitable conversation about why her attitude toward him had changed.

But conversation or not, this morning with Chad had changed everything. Chad was the first man who'd barged through the barricades she'd erected around her body and the first man she'd opened up to since her divorce. Perhaps this was another stage in the healing process. She certainly felt more like her former self—confident, feminine, bold.

Yet there was still a hesitant vestige of caution left over, a lack of trust that hadn't been there before her marriage. However, she couldn't expect all her issues about men to disappear after one incredible lovemaking session with Chad. For now, she would take satisfaction that he had eased some of her old hurts.

He might have charming hands that had woven a spell over her, but he wasn't a magician who could make the past vanish as if it had never been. However, she felt incredibly alive and finally open to enjoying her stay in Eden. Maybe they could try out the recreational activities in the entertainment district, attend a few parties, perhaps even reserve an evening in one of the private rooms. She imagined bringing Chad to the Ravishment Room. The idea of turning the tables on him rushed heat to her face. They could start slowly, perhaps in the Erotica Room, a place rumored to have special oils and soaps, then move on to Purple Passion where the builders had duplicated a Roman bath with exotic mosaic tiles on the walls, ceilings and floors and a tempting purple fountain. At the endless possibilities, she smiled.

After a month with Chad's caring, with his putting her needs first, her heart might be healed as good as new. She twisted her hair into a ponytail, looked in the mirror, then let her hair back down around her shoulders and realized that until now, she'd been avoiding most of her feelings for Chad.

For once in her life, she didn't want to think twice. Not even once. She wanted to go with the flow, enjoy their time together and not analyze it to death.

As she tossed her hairbrush on the vanity and applied a clear lip gloss, she wondered where Chad could be. The house was remarkably quiet. She couldn't hear the television or a stereo or running water from the bathrooms or kitchen. Somehow she didn't think he would be in the exercise room in the basement, but when she descended the stairs, she found the ground floor empty.

Flicking on the lights above the stairs, she headed for the basement, her pulse rate a little higher than normal. She attributed the reaction to finding herself alone rather than to anticipating her reunion with Chad. A quick search downstairs proved fruitless.

She promised herself not to overreact. In Eden, a man didn't abandon his woman or leave them for another. Eden's rules permitted the men free rein of their mistress's grounds, but they weren't allowed to roam over the resort without being accompanied by a woman.

She ascended the stairs to the first floor. Could he have gone for a walk outside?

He was probably lying in the hammock out back, or reading on the porch. She was going to feel silly for worrying even a smidgen over his disappearance once she found him. Brittany climbed the stairs and debated which way to go. Front or back yard?

Before she could decide, an Eden Security Department car parked in front of Samantha's house, soft blue lights flashing. Something was wrong. Was Chad hurt? Gone?

Brittany flung open the front door to find two security guards escorting Chad up the steps.

Chad's sturdy frame looked a little worse for wear. His shirt sported a rip. He had a small cut over one eye, and his knuckles had several raw-looking scrapes that hadn't been there this morning.

"What happened?" Brittany looked into Chad's eyes, hoping he had an explanation that could make all this go away and ease the tight knot of distress in her stomach.

The security guard answered her. "We found him at the hospital."

"The hospital?" Brittany frowned. "Are you hurt?"

"I forgot to fill my prescription before I came to Eden." He stepped away from the guards and toward her. "I need to keep the medicine on hand to fight off occasional bouts of malaria."

The guard shook his head. "He entered the emergency room, pulled shut the curtain and disappeared. Our cameras suffered inexplicable short circuits. We believe he tampered with the wiring. It was only by accident that a nurse found him in the file room."

Chad shrugged nonchalantly. "I was looking for a bathroom."

Brittany wasn't buying his excuse. Again she cautioned herself to hold her emotions in check.

"We think he hacked into the hospital's computer system and made an untraceable phone call, but we can't prove it. So we brought him back to you, ma'am."

The security guards waited as if they expected Brittany to do something. She had no idea what. As the guards' story sank in, she realized that Chad's duplicity was a betrayal of her trust. The tight hold she was keeping on her emotions couldn't withstand the anger that was beginning to suffocate her. Chad had deceived her.

His so-called malaria hadn't been acting up when

he'd carried her upstairs to bed. Nor had the sudden onset of any illness prevented him from an obvious scuffle with the guards.

He was lying.

He'd been intimate with her, then carried her to bed, and while she slept, he'd been up to God knows what. He'd left the house without a note, without a goodbye.

No way did she believe his story. She only knew that once again she felt used, suspecting he'd planned to tire her out so he could escape and then return unnoticed. He'd been slick—no doubt would have gotten away with his scheme—except for a fortuitous accident of being discovered by a nurse.

She didn't bother keeping the anger from her tone. "If you needed to go to the hospital, why didn't you wake me?"

"You needed rest and I figured I'd be back before you woke up. I would have been, too, if these two jokers hadn't decided that looking for the bathroom was a crime." Chad stuck to his story with a dignity that had her doubting the righteousness of her anger. Could he really need a prescription filled to fight off bouts of malaria? It would be like him to take off for the hospital without an explanation just as he'd taken off from the dance floor in search of a safety pin.

"Ma'am, he's violated his contract under paragraph D, section four. If you want to kick him out, we can pack his things and escort him to the gate. You need never see him again."

She crossed her arms over her chest, tempted to do

just that. Eden was supposed to be her vacation. She didn't need this kind of aggravation.

"I can explain," Chad told her.

"Then do so."

"We need to be alone."

Being alone with him was the last thing she wanted. She didn't trust herself. He'd make his explanations and she'd believe him, because she wanted to. She shook her head, ignoring her aching heart and the cold that coated her like frost. "It's better to make a clean break."

"I'm not Devlin," Chad snapped back. "I didn't betray you."

Then why did she hurt as if he had? Why did she feel as though every cell in her body wanted to weep with sadness and frustration and anger? And why did she want to fling herself into Chad's arms and let him talk her into keeping him for a month? Because what she'd regained with him was too precious to lose. He'd given her back a measure of her self-esteem, and though he'd hurt her with his lies, she owed him.

Brittany always paid her debts. She ignored Chad and nodded to the guards. "Leave him with me."

"Thank you for being willing to listen," Chad told her, his blue eyes serious.

The guards departed, seemingly not the least bit surprised by her decision. She supposed they'd seen men break the rules before.

Brittany waited, hoping Chad would give her an explanation of his own accord. Despite doubts, she hadn't really bought his phony story and hoped he'd volunteer the truth.

"What were you doing in the hospital files?" she asked him as they walked up the stairs. She gestured for him to sit on a bench on the wide front porch. Instead he seated himself on the steps and patted the spot beside him.

She wondered if he realized that she didn't want him back in the house, not until he'd satisfied her curiosity. Nevertheless, she took the seat next to him, careful not to touch, careful not to lean into his heat.

"I came to Eden on a mission," Chad told her. "The security guards were correct that I used the phone. I had to call a superior to obtain permission to reveal this information to you."

"Those phones take special codes to use an outside line."

"A SEAL is taught how to bypass codes. I called Admiral Gates and he gave me permission to confide in you."

"Terrific." She let out a long, low sigh of frustration. Chad was going to spin one fantastic story where she couldn't check the facts. "So what's your mission?"

"The admiral's son, Lyle, came to Eden."

"So? Daddy doesn't want his son to be bought by a woman?"

"Lyle never came back."

Brittany frowned in confusion. "What do you mean he never came back? When was his contract up?"

"Six months ago."

"Maybe someone extended it." Brittany didn't understand the gravity in Chad's tone. "Maybe he left Eden and never called home."

"The admiral doesn't think so."

If Lyle wanted to stay in Eden, why should Chad be so concerned? He sounded grim and determined.

"My mission is to find Lyle, talk to him and ultimately reunite him with his father."

Great. Not only was Chad here under false pretenses, he wouldn't care if he broke every rule in Eden's book to accomplish his mission for a son who probably didn't want to be found. "Maybe Lyle wants to stay here."

"I don't think so."

"Maybe he needs the money. Maybe he finds the work pleasurable. Maybe he fell in love."

"I need to find out. Right now, I'm only sure Lyle fell from Laurel's window."

"How do you know that?"

"Francois likes to talk. He heard it from one of the long-timers and told me."

"It could be a rumor."

"A SEAL with Lyle's training wouldn't fall out a window."

"You think he was pushed by an eighty-year-old wheelchair-bound, retired Supreme Court justice?" She rolled her eyes at the sky, thinking Chad had missed his calling and should have written for the daytime soaps.

"I figured he might have ended up in the hospital."

That's why Chad had sneaked into the file room, for the medical record. "Did Lyle suffer injuries?"

"His file says he's dead."

"What?" The news, given in a flinty tone but tempered with the hard steel of his seriousness, made her shiver.

"There's even a death certificate."

A chill shivered down her spine. "You think someone pushed this man out a window, took him to the hospital where he died and no one bothered to inform his next of kin?"

"It gets better."

She braced herself for more bad news. Chad smiled grimly through tightly pressed lips. "The death certificate was dated two months ago, but I think I saw Lyle at the masquerade."

Another mystery cleared up, and her instincts had been dead on. "So you weren't looking for a safety pin any more than you needed a prescription to fight off malaria?"

"Afraid not."

Frustration rumbled up from her chest and recoiled on her tongue. "You're a damn good liar."

"There's no need for me to lie to you again."

His look was gentle, and it scared her that she believed him, scared her enough for sarcasm to blurt from her mouth undiluted. "Yes, I know the admiral gave you permission to tell all."

"Only to you. You must keep this conversation confidential."

She shook her head, wary of keeping his secrets. "I never agreed to that."

He turned to face her and, taking her icy hands in his warm ones, knelt on a step below her feet so their gazes met at the same level. "If you talk to anyone, they'll kick me out of here so fast, we won't have a chance to investigate."

"Whoa! There is no *we*. You're acting alone here, pal."

"I'd like your help."

"I'm sure you would. You also want me to keep quiet, and I don't like it."

"Don't you get it? If someone is covering up Lyle's death, he was murdered. If that someone finds out I'm trying to uncover the crime, I might find myself as dead as Lyle."

"And if I help you, I could end up dead, too." She knew Chad wouldn't ever let her risk her life. He was doing whatever it took to convince her to remain silent. "You don't think Lyle's dead."

"I don't. I think I saw him that night."

"You're scaring me."

He pulled her into his arms. "As long as you don't confide in anyone, we'll both be safe."

He was about to kiss her. She could tell from the blue flames in his eyes and she pulled back. "If I send you away, we'll both be safe, too."

"Is that what you want?"

Why was he asking her that question? Did he think she didn't know her own mind?

Maybe she didn't.

Eden was supposed to be a romantic adventure. Instead she had to deal with all these feelings and emotions that she wished would go away. If Chad's suspicions were correct, someone in Eden had committed a murder and gotten away with it. She couldn't just pretend she hadn't heard about a possible crime. She'd never really approved of Eden before she'd come here, and now that she'd seen the resort, she had difficulty believing anything sinister had happened here. Yet there were many things she hadn't become comfortable with—such as owning a man for a month. On the other hand her mother had a lot invested in the resort, so she felt compelled to find out the truth.

Now she had to decide whether to believe Chad. She still wasn't sure she could trust him but wanted to take the time to find out. If she had to play along, pretend to believe his story, to find out what exactly was happening between them, then she would.

It should have been a difficult decision.

It wasn't.

She should be calling security to remove him from the premises.

She didn't.

She wasn't about to deny herself the pleasure of keeping his company for a month. Not when she was already looking forward to kissing him again. Especially since she couldn't help but be pleased that he hadn't come to Eden for sex and money. He'd come here on a mission, and until he found Lyle, she really wouldn't be able to evaluate whether Chad was staying with her out of convenience, lust, or because a true affinity existed between them.

However, helping him with his mission was different from pretending to turn a blind eye to his activities. She was still wary. No way did she trust him one hundred percent yet. She looked at his face and considered the possibilities. Was something diabolical going on in Eden? If so, wouldn't it be wrong to pretend she knew nothing? Didn't she owe it to her mother and her friends to investigate—if only to prove Chad's suspicions wrong?

Those other reasons aside, how could she not help him? Especially when, if she sent him away, she'd never learn the truth about whether or not they were as good together as she thought. She needed to know if she could trust Chad but, even more important, she needed to know if her judgment had improved over time.

Brittany vowed to use this month with Chad to explore her sensuality, to find out who she really wanted to be. Either way, when she left Eden she'd be a different person, a healed woman, a stronger woman. She could test herself with Chad, see if she could overcome the mistakes of her past, but she had to remain careful. Once before, she'd trusted a man too easily—she wouldn't repeat her mistake. This time she wanted a man who would prove himself to her, and to do that, she had to give them time together.

"How can I help?"

He grinned, clearly surprised and delighted by her decision, but keeping in character with his tough-guy

SEAL image, he tried to look cool and feign he hadn't doubted her loyalty for a second. "You can pretend to be madly in love with me."

She licked her bottom lip. "I can do that."

"Pretend you want to show me off."

"Shouldn't be too difficult."

"Pretend you want to go to the public areas and restaurants and parties."

"So you can look for Lyle?"

He mouth swooped down on hers. "That, too."

CHAD CONSIDERED HIMSELF a lucky man for a variety of reasons. When those security men had caught him in the hospital, he'd figured he was dog meat and he'd be lucky to be thrown out on his ass without someone putting him in a cell or taking legal action or worse. He'd certainly never expected Brittany to forgive him or to be escorting her to dinner at Laurel's house that evening. However he knew he was treading on dangerous ground. Brittany still didn't trust him, but he would prove himself to her.

She'd surprised him by allowing him to stay. He'd surprised himself when he'd kissed her on the steps and had to restrain himself. What had started out as a straightforward mission had turned complicated. There was far more to Brittany than the chilly surface with which she faced the world. Brittany's staunch support reminded him of his friends in the military, individuals he considered the backbone of America. She liked the appearance of orderliness and tidiness in her life. She might not be sentimental or gushy, and played her feelings close to the vest, but she had an innate loyalty about her that he was learning he could count on. Although she was careful not to give in to reckless abandon or wild excess, once he pushed her past her comfort zone, she threw away all that careful self-discipline.

And he'd adored making her lose control, watching her emerge from a cocoon and spread her wings. It couldn't have been easy for her to agree to help him and not say a word to Samantha, but once she'd decided, she'd arranged a whirlwind of social plans, accepting a last-minute dinner invitation from Laurel.

As they arrived, Chad hoped he'd get an opportunity to speak with the ex Supreme Court justice alone, or perhaps a maid or gardener, to question them about Lyle's fall from Laurel's window. A house this size should have servants, probably a chef and a butler, too. The ostentatious three-story mansion was constructed of gray stone and sported three chimneys jutting out from its steeply pitched roof. Party goers could be seen through etched-glass front doors that a butler opened to greet arriving guests.

As they walked into the mansion's foyer, he realized that while he'd envisioned an intimate dinner for maybe six or eight, Laurel must have invited over ten couples. The high-ceilinged foyer sported a teardrop chandelier, elegant cherry paneling and was decorated in surprisingly good taste with fine art, antiques and several gilded mirrors.

"I expected rhinestones dripping from the wallpaper," Chad whispered in Brittany's delectably shaped ear as he helped himself to two glasses of spiced wine and handed her one.

Brittany had worn gold-hooped earrings and a spaghetti-strapped dress that showed off her figure and revealed more cleavage than he would have liked. As Francois and Aurora separated themselves from the group milling in the huge front hall and joined them, Francois seemed overly interested in Brittany.

Francois picked up Brittany's hand and kissed it as he eyed her chest. "Good evening."

Aurora shot a ten-thousand-dollar-a-day grin at Brittany. "Forgive his bad manners. He's trying to make me jealous."

"And am I succeeding?" Francois asked her without the least bit of embarrassment at being caught or held accountable.

Chad chuckled, leaned forward and kissed Aurora hello on the cheek, taking the opportunity to whisper loudly enough into her ear so that both Brittany and Francois could hear him. "Give the guy a break."

Aurora winked at Brittany. "I've given him *more* than a break."

"That's so true, but she's still holding back on me."

"Francois, really. You've enjoyed every inch of me."

At Aurora's casual mention of sex, Brittany's face flushed a little, but Chad also spied a gleam of amusement in her eyes. He would have given a month's pay to have read her thoughts.

"You've held back the most important part of yourself," Francois complained.

"Really?" Chad asked, draining his wine in a swallow and leaving his glass on a sideboard.

"She's holding back her heart." Francois frowned at Aurora. "I've given you everything…and you want to throw me over for a man who won't appreciate your true beauty, your brilliant intelligence, your sparkling wit."

Aurora chuckled. "Don't be so melodramatic."

"I thought you'd bought Francois's services for the month?" Brittany asked.

"I did. If he doesn't behave himself I may trade him in for two twenty-year-olds."

"Ha," Francois retorted in a huff. "You think you can take on two men? You can't even handle me."

Chad could tell their bickering was already like a married couple who clearly adored each other. Despite her goading, Aurora couldn't seem to stop touching Francois.

Laurel rolled up in her wheelchair to meet them like a queen on her throne. Tonight she'd dressed in purple. At least he assumed there was purple fabric beneath the purple feathers with amethyst rhinestones. A cigar in her mouth, she greeted her guests and asked everyone to join her in the dining room for an informal buffet.

Chad squeezed Brittany's hand, their prearranged signal for her to hang in the crowd while he investigated. She should be safe enough. He'd told her to keep her ears open but leave the questioning to him.

He didn't want her to call attention to herself or subject herself to the slightest danger. He believed her to be safe among the group of party goers, yet he'd warned her to be extra careful about what she said.

The moment he left her, he saw Aurora drawing her into the study for a private conversation. He wondered if Aurora could have heard about his altercation with the security guards at the hospital and intended to grill Brittany. More likely, she wanted the details of their love life.

Either way, he knew he could count on Brittany to keep their secrets. He only wished they'd had a few more to keep. Because sometime between his coming to Eden and this afternoon when she'd agreed to help him, Chad had decided he wanted more from Brittany than one afternoon of love play.

As he slipped up the stairs in hopes of finding a servant to question, Chad forced his mind back to his mission. He couldn't afford to get caught again—not here, where Lyle had gone out a window.

He needed answers and that necessitated taking some risks. He could minimize his jeopardy by taking every precaution. So he moved quickly, an excuse ready on his tongue if someone suddenly confronted him.

He climbed the steps rapidly and headed down a dark hall. Chatter and soft music from the party below filtered up to the second story. When someone switched on a light in a room down the hall, he reached for a doorknob and ducked into a bedroom.

SLIGHTLY NERVOUS OVER Chad's reconnaissance mission upstairs, Brittany was happy for Aurora distracting her. She kept expecting an alarm to go off and guards to come running, but she set aside her barely touched wineglass, pasted a smile on her face and followed Aurora into the music room, hoping that nothing would go wrong.

A glossy white baby grand piano dominated the room. Soft carpets and muted lighting set a pleasant ambience for private conversation.

"I was hoping you might be able to help me with Samantha," Brittany confided to Aurora, hoping to head off a conversation about Francois that she sensed was coming. She didn't feel comfortable giving Aurora advice about her love life, not when she'd messed up her own marriage, not when she didn't know what she felt about Chad.

"Your mom?"

"Yeah. I never see her with anyone in Eden. I thought I'd pick out someone for her."

"You mean turn the tables?"

"I want her to be happy. She's always alone. Always worrying over me."

"And if you find her someone, she'll have less time to check up on you," Aurora guessed shrewdly.

"Exactly. Do you know anyone she might like?"

Aurora frowned, seemingly not the least bit concerned about wrinkling her spectacular skin. "I can't be sure of Samantha's tastes. She's rather a free spirit, isn't she?"

"I'd appreciate it if you could ask Francois. Chad

said he socialized with the men and might know someone suitable."

Aurora raised an eyebrow. "Suitable? That's an interesting word choice," she said.

Brittany stiffened and was ready to head for the door, but then Aurora took her hand. "Forgive me, I'm not thinking straight. Of course, I'll ask Francois. If we're still speaking." Aurora twisted her hands. "I've made a terrible mistake."

"What kind of mistake?" Brittany took a seat on the piano bench while the agitated model paced.

"I should have read Francois's file."

"Isn't it a little late for that?" Brittany asked wryly.

"Exactly my point. I thought he was a…a…"

"Bimbo?"

Aurora threw her hands up in the air. "He was supposed to be a body."

"Every man is more than a body."

"He was supposed to be a sex machine without a brain."

"He's not a sex machine?" Brittany teased.

"He's smart."

"And that's your big problem?"

Aurora dropped her hands to her sides in disgust. "He's a student. He's going to be a doctor. The money he's earning here will help pay for medical school."

"So?"

Aurora stopped pacing and sighed. "So, I like him. A lot. A lot more than I'd planned."

"I'm having the same problem with Chad," Brittany confided.

"Maybe we should send them both back into the pool?" Aurora suggested.

Brittany shook her head, knowing better. Even while they spoke, she constantly worried about Chad's safety upstairs. "You really think if the men are out of sight, they'll be out of our minds?"

## 10

CHAD HAD EXPECTED the upstairs bedroom to be empty. Instead he found himself looking at a well-preserved fifty-year-old man standing on a wind-sailing board with a kiddie rig sail in the middle of an otherwise empty room. A fan blew the man's long bleached-blond hair back from his face and the smooth melody of the Beach Boys played on a tape machine.

Chad grinned at the would-be sailor, hoping who-ever he was might want to chat. "Sorry, I was looking for—"

"Come in. Come in. I'm all done practicing my tacking and jibing." The man, wearing an Hawaiian shirt and baggy surfer shorts, stepped off the board that he'd propped onto bricks to prevent the skeg from breaking, shut off the fan and held out his hand for Chad to shake. "I'm Alf Barber."

"Chad Hunter."

"One of Laurel's lost guests?"

"Not so lost," Chad admitted, taking in the man's eyes as he removed dark sunglasses. Alf might be dreaming of Hawaiian surf in his bedroom, but keen intelligence shone from his eyes. Chad recognized the man's yearning for the sea and sought to capitalize on their shared passion. "I joined the navy and became a SEAL because I love the sea."

"Ever wind-sail?"

"No, but I've surfed Maui's north shore."

"Cool. Would you like a brew?" Alf reached into a cooler and handed Chad a bottle.

"Thanks." Chad twisted off the cap. "I came up here to see the spot where another sea buddy, a SEAL, dropped out of one of these upstairs windows."

Alf gestured over his shoulder with his thumb. "You picked the right room. It was that window."

Chad approached the window and examined it carefully. The sill was too high for a man to fall out accidentally. In addition it would take a good amount of strength to open it, and he doubted Laurel could have done so from a wheelchair.

Chad frowned. "He must have had a few too many brewskies. How could anyone accidentally fall out from—"

"Oh, it was no accident."

Had Lyle been pushed? Perhaps by another man? Perhaps by Alf, whose arms looked as though he lifted weights on his nights off from wind sailing in the bedroom.

Chad hid his suspicions behind a mild tone. "What happened?"

Alf sipped his beer. "Lyle was escaping down a rope. Laurel caught him and cut the rope with a knife. Lyle fell and ended up in the hospital."

"How do you know?" Chad asked.

"I'm Laurel's nurse. She's not as self-sufficient as she appears."

"Really?"

"It's a sweet deal. She only needs me in the morning and again at night. The rest of the day I do pretty much as I please."

"You wouldn't happen to know why Lyle was fleeing out the window instead of using the stairs, would you?" Chad asked curiously.

"He was sneaking out to meet a woman." Alf shrugged. "It's no big secret, although Laurel wouldn't want me talking about it."

"I'll keep the information between us sea dogs," Chad promised. "Did the woman have a name?"

Alf downed half his beer and then frowned at Chad with suspicion. "You sure are curious."

Chad didn't deny his more-than-casual interest. "Like I said, I'm a SEAL, too. It's part of the code, like sailors who race across the ocean but stop to help other vessels in trouble. We try and look out for one another."

"It's a little late for that. I wasn't here that night, but Lyle ended up at the hospital. He was lucky he didn't break his neck."

"He had a spinal injury?"

"No. Like a cat, he landed on his feet and rolled. The docs set his broken arm and he's as good as new."

Broken arm? As good as new? Then Lyle hadn't died from the fall as the medical file in the hospital reported, firming up Chad's suspicion that he'd seen Lyle the night of the masquerade.

"So what happened, then?"

"Laurel threw one of her fits. It wasn't pleasant, I'll tell you that. When the woman gets mad, she throws things. Worse is the insults she hurls at her staff."

"Why do they stay?" Chad asked, already knowing the answer but wanting a chance to think. He needed the name of the woman Lyle had been trying to see that night.

"The money's good. Another three years and I can buy my own island and spend my days sailing in real surf."

"Try Hawaii. The wind is always up and so are the waves. The beaches are better than advertised. I wonder if Lyle took off for the sea. You ever see him after he left the hospital?"

"Sure. Lots of times." Bingo. That was the confirmation he needed to confirm that Lyle hadn't died here in Eden. There had been no murder, no death—only an elaborate cover-up. "That sailor was real popular with the ladies."

"They say it's the uniform." Chad shrugged, wondering why a cover-up was needed. Had Lyle expected someone to come looking for him? Or could the hospital file have been a mistake? "So which lucky lady bought him next?"

"The model." Alf snapped his fingers. "I don't recall her last name, but her first is Aurora."

"Lyle must have been happy to be with Aurora after—"

"I wouldn't know," Alf interrupted, sipping more of his beer. "The odd thing is as eager as Lyle was to get out of here, I never saw him often with Aurora."

"You go to a lot of parties?"

"Laurel entertains a lot and I hear things. No one saw Aurora together with Lyle much after his accident."

"Maybe they spent their time in private," Chad suggested, "or swimming in the lake. Lyle's an excellent swimmer."

"Aurora was partying every night, hanging out with different guys. People talk about a beautiful woman like her, but I never heard that she was with Lyle."

Chad rubbed his chin in confusion. "What are you saying?"

"I'm not sure. I never thought about it much, but for a man to break the rules and climb out the window for a lady must mean he wanted her real bad. If Lyle got what he wanted with Aurora, then why would the lady be with different men night after night?"

"Maybe Aurora likes having several men at once?"

"Others maybe. Not her."

Chad shelved the puzzle of Aurora for now. "I'd like to look him up while I'm here. Have you seen Lyle recently?"

"Not in the last two weeks."

"Is there a registry anywhere?"

"None that I know of, but he liked to hang out in the private rooms. As I recall, he seemed to have a particular fancy for the Fetish Room."

Chad talked a little more about the sea, thanked Alf for the beer and found his way back to Brittany. Alf had given him much to think about.

In addition to hoping to speak with Brittany to fill her in on what he'd learned, he wanted to ask Aurora about Lyle. When Chad found Brittany at the buffet line, she was talking to Samantha. Actually, she was talking about a good-looking guy. That Brittany thought so highly of him, and was telling her mother so, pleased him.

The more time he spent with Brittany, the more he appreciated her good sense. She'd accepted his mission and even covered for him while he'd investigated upstairs. And she was letting go of the pain from her past, letting her feminine potency reemerge. He was looking forward to exploring the private rooms with Brittany with the perfectly good excuse that he expected Lyle to show up there.

Chad joined the women, coming up beside Brittany in time to hear her say, "He's handsome and has good manners. What's not to like?"

Handsome? Okay, Chad was glad to know Brittany liked his looks. However, she made him sound insipid when she spoke about his manners. After what they'd shared, he really thought she could do better with her praise.

"I'd prefer we dropped the subject," Samantha

told her daughter with a sharp tone that she probably used to make her employees jump to her bidding.

"Mom, you don't object to his mustache, do you? I think it's kind of cute."

Chad frowned in confusion. He'd assumed Brittany had been talking about him, not another man.

"MOTHER, I DON'T UNDERSTAND why you won't at least have dinner with Charles. Laurel said she thought you would like him," Brittany told Samantha as Chad joined them in the dining room. She kept talking to Samantha about finding her a date, but her stomach settled with relief at seeing Chad back downstairs, seemingly none the worse for his snooping.

"Laurel judges men by the firmness of their butts." Samantha chuckled in amusement over her wine. "My criteria are somewhat more—"

"More what?" Laurel asked as she blew cigar smoke at Samantha.

To her mother's credit, she didn't even blink. "More varied."

"Is that so?" Laurel reached toward Chad's butt, but he was on to her now and edged away.

Brittany took his arm and together they escaped the two women who continued to bicker over the merits of imaginary dates. She failed to understand why her mother came here so often if she didn't avail herself of the possibilities.

Brittany almost laughed at herself. One week ago, her mother had dragged her here. Now she wanted to find her mother a man. Brittany might not totally approve of Eden and the concept behind it, but she did love her mother and hated for her to spend so much time alone. Ever since Samantha's affair with the sculptor, Jeffrey, she'd never dated the same man for more than a night. Now Brittany wanted her mother to find someone. It was as if their opinions about Eden had somewhat reversed. Brittany knew her change of heart and mind had everything to do with the man by her side, but once again she reminded herself to be wary. Chad had lied to her twice and she would be a fool not to think he might do so again. Until she knew him better, until he solved the mystery of Lyle's disappearance, she needed to remain uncommitted, open-minded, and stay alert to the dangers.

"Find anything interesting?" Brittany asked as they moved through the buffet line, loading their plates from silver servers, then heading toward tables arranged in intimate circles around the room.

"Did I find anything interesting? How about a damsel in need of her escort's attention?"

"I meant..." She glanced upstairs.

"Let's eat and say goodbye early."

A half hour later Brittany and Chad departed Laurel's party, and he was finally free to tell her what he'd learned. Laurel's home sat on a grand hill close to Eden's entertainment district, and Chad steered Brittany toward the many restaurants, private rooms and parties held there that dominated the nighttime activities.

They walked along a sidewalk hand in hand, comfortable with each other in a way that reminded Brittany of a couple who'd known each other much longer than a few days. Eden had been designed by experts for intimate walks and quiet conversations, and the resort worked to seduce the occupants on many levels. It was private and intimate. No one judged anyone. If Brittany happened to make a fool over herself because of Chad, no one in the outside world would ever know. Protected from the press, from the judgment of friends and fellow associates, she had let herself relax with Chad in a way that wouldn't have been possible outside this haven.

Sometimes she wondered how much more she could accomplish, how much more she would be able to feel, if she weren't afraid to fail. The past few years, she'd hidden, closed herself off like an injured animal licking her wounds.

Well, the pain had subsided and, while she might have scars, Brittany was ready to come out of hiding. More important, she was ready to trust her instincts again.

As they left Laurel's house behind, the sounds of music and laughter diminished. Brittany squeezed Chad's hand. "What did you find out?"

"I ran into Laurel's nurse, Alf. He's seen Lyle since the date on the hospital file that declared Lyle dead."

"So you were right. He's still alive." Her heart lifted, glad they weren't investigating a murder.

"Apparently Lyle was climbing out Laurel's window to meet Aurora."

"Aurora's with Francois now, so she may not know Lyle's current whereabouts."

"I'd still like to ask Aurora a few questions, but it'll have to wait. Apparently they left the party earlier than we did."

"Is Lyle here in Eden?" she asked.

"Alf hasn't seen him in almost two weeks."

"So when do you think he disappeared?"

"I think I saw him the night of the masquerade. No one I've talked to has seen him since."

"It was really him?"

"I'm not sure. I didn't get a good look."

She tilted her head and glanced at him in the moonlight. "You think the timing of his disappearance is a coincidence?"

"I don't know. He may not have disappeared—we just might not have run into him. Eden's a big place." He paused, then continued. "Then again, Alf may be misinformed. Lyle may have sustained a head injury during that fall and suffered amnesia or a personality change. Although it's more likely he recognized me and went into hiding."

"Why?"

"He probably knows the admiral wants him back home and once he saw me...well, it wouldn't be hard for him to figure out that the admiral sent me."

"Makes sense."

She and Chad had more questions than ever that needed answering, but he seemed determined to solve the puzzle. "I'd love to know who altered the medical file and why."

"Maybe Lyle did it after you recognized him," she suggested.

"To make me think I'd been mistaken at seeing him at the masquerade and believe him dead and give up? You may be right."

Brittany squeezed his hand. "I hope we find him soon."

"Me, too." He paused. "But why did Laurel risk cutting that rope as he climbed out the window?"

"Because he betrayed her. This is a small community and while the employees are paid well not to gossip, the guests do talk. She had to have been angry and embarrassed that he'd tried to leave her."

Chad considered her words before speaking. "She could have been accused of murder, especially with a medical file in the hospital stating he'd died from the fall she'd caused. It's hard to believe an ex Supreme Court justice would resort to such an extreme."

"Laurel's still a woman. You simply don't understand how painful and embarrassing it can be to be betrayed by someone you love."

"There's no indication that Laurel loved...we aren't talking about Laurel and Lyle, are we?"

"I guess not."

"This is about you and Devlin?"

Brittany took in a clean breath of the fresh night air and plunged ahead. She'd told him about discovering Devlin's treachery before, but now she wanted him to know all the details. She wanted to share the most awful moment of her life with Chad. "I came home early from work and found Devlin in my bed, on my sheets, making love to another woman.''

''It must have been horrible.''

''I've never told anyone the worst part.''

Chad stopped walking and folded her against his chest. ''You don't have to relive it.''

''I've kept that day bottled up inside so long, I think it's been poisoning me.''

''Then spill it.''

She took comfort in the gentleness of his tone, the heat of his arms around her, the protective sound of his heart beating by her ear. ''Devlin was having sex with Vanessa Wainwright, my best friend.''

''God! I'm so sorry.'' Chad hugged her close, smoothed his fingers over her hair and down her back. He didn't ask questions, but held her until her trembling stopped and she felt strong enough to go on.

''It was a double betrayal and I never saw it coming. Vanessa and I had been friends since sixth grade. I spent Christmas at her house, she spent Easter at mine. She was the first person I told when I lost my virginity. I was maid of honor at her wedding. I'm godmother to her daughter. But Vanessa was competitive—she always wanted to win. It wasn't good enough that we were both cheerleaders—she had to be captain. Her wedding had to be more lavish than mine. She had to be happier, thinner, richer. It took me so long to see that she hadn't ever been a real friend. She was jealous. She had to have what I had. Eventually she wasn't satisfied until she had my husband, too.''

"You never told Samantha?"

"I was too humiliated. You see, until that moment, I'd thought Devlin the perfect man. I thought I had the perfect life. A career, a fine husband, I had it all, and I was convinced I deserved it because I was a good girl and played by the rules."

"Life doesn't work that way."

"So I found out." She pulled herself together and leaned back to look at Chad. "Devlin must have dumped Vanessa almost immediately. He followed up with a very public string of affairs—a different woman on his arm every night. He went to the same parties we'd always gone to."

"You stayed home and hid?"

"I threw myself into my work, but it was my way of hiding. The very worst part was that I no longer trusted—"

"Men? Women?"

"Myself."

"I suppose that's understandable when the two people you love betray you."

The pain was still there, but no longer as sharp. The memories had receded to a dull ache that she hoped would disappear completely with time. She wanted to put the past behind her and she felt ready to more on, move forward. Talking to Chad made her feel better. His arms around her helped more than he could know.

She couldn't help wondering about Chad though. He'd told her about his marriage and divorce but hadn't given her any details. "What about your divorce? What extra baggage do you carry around?"

Chad sighed. "Our divorce was my fault. A wife has a right to expect her man to come home at night."

"Lots of men travel in their work."

"Most have regular schedules. With my job, I couldn't even phone to let her know when she could expect me. Sometimes, I had to leave without even saying goodbye and could be out of contact for hours, days or weeks. It wasn't fair to ask Roxy to live for the times I could be with her. We tried to make the marriage work, but she finally gave up and divorced me."

"And since then?"

"No one serious. I won't take that kind of guilt trip or repeat the same mistake. I never meant to hurt Roxy. I know better than to try again."

"What a pair we are," she said casually enough, but suppressed a little disappointment at his not ever planning to get involved again—especially if she wanted to follow through on her feelings for Chad.

"We make a fine pair, and I suspect we're well matched in passion." His voice changed from protective to seductive. "Alf also told me that Lyle likes to hang out in the private rooms. I'm thinking that we should stake them out."

"In the interest of your investigation?" She trailed one nail lightly down his cheek, heat already gathering in her lower torso.

"It's a hard job, but someone has to do it."

Her hand drifted below his waist. "The job isn't the only hard thing around here."

CHAD KNEW from the literature he'd read that Eden's entertainment district was the heart and soul of the resort. He'd never expected to be so eager to explore it with the woman who had bought his contract. Ever since she'd learned about his search for Lyle, he'd felt like part of a team.

Working with Brittany was as satisfying as working with Red Squad, a group of men to whom he had trusted his life. As partners went, she contributed when she could, let him take the lead when necessary and didn't complain about hardships—like being abandoned at a dinner party. In addition, she seemed as eager to push their relationship to the next level as he was.

He felt no guilt. She knew the score, knew he wasn't the kind of man to commit, knew he wasn't husband material and that this was supposed to be his vacation. He saw no harm in having a good time during his mission, especially when she was so obviously enjoying his company, too.

He and Brittany strolled toward the complex. Although anticipation of making love to Brittany had him wired, he couldn't help being impressed by the these public areas and the sophistication of the planning that had gone into the construction.

Bubbling fountains and man-made moonlight lit up the sculptures that decorated the immaculate grounds designed for window shopping, dining and entertainment. The choices were both casual and elegant, the dining facilities offering everything from take-out pizza to five-star French cuisine. For those seeking informal entertainment, he spied a bowling alley, a movie theater, a playhouse, a pool hall with the latest in video games, pinball machines and Ping-Pong tables.

"It's a city."

"There's more." Brittany tugged him onto a broad avenue that lacked all vehicles except golf carts. "The best is yet to come. We can window-shop for a private room."

She spoke boldly, eager to share the night with him, and he realized that his coaxing had released her from her self-imposed imprisonment. Beside him walked a passionate woman who knew her own mind, and he couldn't wait to taste her again, touch her again, hear her soft moans of need. Only this time he fully intended to be deep inside her when she screamed his name.

Chad spied a marquee and, distracted from his thoughts of making love to Brittany, his mouth dropped open at the variety of possibilities. There were rooms to celebrate the holidays 24/7/365. One window displayed a Christmas Room with a Santa, fake snow and his helper dressed in a suggestive red costume. The Valentine Room sported a red heart-shaped whirlpool. The Fourth of July Room promised a holographic fireworks display hot enough to burn.

The windows seemed to be grouped in topics. After they passed holidays, food came next. A Chocolate

Room, a Honey Pot Room, the Bakery and the Confection Room. To entice customers, the management vented mouthwatering scents of chocolate and strawberries into the air.

"See anything you like?" Brittany asked with a mischievous grin.

"I feel like a kid in a toy shop." He spun her into his arms and looked into her eyes, dark with passion, her cheeks rosy from the night air. "But what looks best is you."

She licked her bottom lip. "Good answer. You don't look so bad yourself." She reached up and tried to pull his head down. "Kiss me."

"I won't go there until we have a private room, because I might not be able to stop."

She laughed, tucked her arm through his, and they kept walking.

The history section seemed very popular. The Victorian Room could have been furnished right out of a museum, while the Pirate Room promised authenticity with the rolling action of waves and the accompanying sounds of the sea. Most rooms took on a decidedly romantic bent, but there was also a War Room, an Underground Bunker and a Tank. Something for every taste, he supposed.

The fourth section advertised nature. A Rose Garden, a Forest, a Desert complete with tent, camels and sheik costumes. The Rain Forest guaranteed warm showers and the Caribbean Room showed a poster of an aquamarine sea and powder-white beaches.

Brittany watched his reactions to the advertisements with a glint of amusement in her eyes that couldn't quite hide her impatience to make a decision. "Some rooms are large hotel suites, other have their own buildings."

"For privacy?" he asked,

"That and climate control. Keeping a rain forest indoors has its own technical problems. There's supposed to be an Underwater Room where one has to swim down past a glass wall of sharks to a sealed-off chamber."

"Swimming isn't exactly what I have in mind right now." Chad watched her lips part and her pupils dilate and thought they really should make a selection soon.

"There's only one more section but—"

"But what?"

"Those rooms are more...unusual."

"We don't have to—"

"We should at least look. This section appeals to those with more unique tastes and includes the Fetish Room. We could see if it's booked for the night."

"If it's not, want me to make a reservation?" he teased.

She slapped his arm. "Forget it. Let's go back. Besides, the computer system won't tell us if Lyle booked the room. Privacy is guarded."

"But since Alf said Lyle hangs out around the Fetish Room, we can find out when that room will next be free, right?"

"I suppose."

She sounded reluctant, and he couldn't resist teasing her again. "We can rent the room next door—the Bondage Room."

"If I didn't know you so well, I'd hit you. But I'd probably hurt my hand."

He chuckled. "When the couple's time is up, we can watch to see who comes out."

"You want to spy?"

"Observe."

Disappointment clouded her eyes. "But…"

"Come on. Once we figure out how long the room is tied up we needn't stay next door. We can pick any room and go enjoy ourselves."

Chad walked toward one of the computer terminals set between the window advertisements. He typed in his name and was surprised to see a huge credit beside his name. "Where did all this money come from?"

"Samantha, I'm sure. She wants us to have a good time."

Her mother was complex. She threatened him openly, then deposited cash in his account. The soft glove and the big stick—she was obviously a woman accustomed to getting her way. He wondered briefly if she was alone or had some man stashed for the night in the hotel where she was staying.

Chad quickly moved to the next screen on the monitor and chose the Fetish Room. "It's booked until noon tomorrow."

"Good." Brittany looked pleased. "That means I can have you all to myself until then."

"You certainly can." He hugged her against his

side and flipped to a screen that gave them options for tonight. "You have any preferences?"

She raised an eyebrow and said dauntlessly, "Surprise me."

# 11

BRITTANY HAD HEARD people in Eden praise the private rooms, but she never expected such hedonistic extravagance inside them. Over her lifetime, she had grown accustomed to the eccentricities and opulence of the wealthy. Her mother's friends spent money as easily as they breathed. In addition, the biggest donors to her foundation often headed Fortune 500 companies and lived in the lap of lavishness. But the decor here—granite columns and soaring arches, flowing fountains with platinum spigots and expensive art—seemed decadent. Many of the women who'd built Eden gave generously to her foundation, and very deliberately she thrust out of her mind how many hungry children could have been fed with the funds put into constructing this dome.

Long ago, she'd learned to partition her life into segments. She didn't hold it against people for living well or enjoying the fruits of their labors. She wouldn't feel guilty for taking this time with Chad to enjoy herself as they walked through the Starlight Room's entrance.

Plush white carpeting lined the floors and ceilings, and lavish black-and-silver wallpaper interspersed with mirrors decorated the walls. Tables were all chrome and glass, sparkling like glitter without a speck of dust. The futuristic decor of the entranceway could have been cold but, instead, created an atmosphere of otherworldliness.

After Chad had made his choice of the Starlight Room and they'd entered the building, he'd whispered in Brittany's ear, "See you soon," before male and female attendants ushered them off to separate changing rooms.

If she was to have doubts about making love to Chad, now was the time they would haunt her. Without his presence to shore up her determination, she walked slowly down the hallway, wondering if nerves and hesitation would come.

They didn't.

In fact, she was pleased to discover only eager anticipation in her heart. Hunger for Chad had her on edge but in the most vital and elemental of ways. She wanted to savor her anticipation, and she couldn't help quickening her step to match the accelerated beat of her heart.

She wanted Chad.

She wanted his hands on her body.

She wanted him over her and under her. Inside her.

And most of all she wanted to explore the long-term possibilities. She understood he didn't believe that could happen due to his career. No matter how badly her marriage had ended, no matter how many of her illusions Devlin had shattered, she still thought that a couple could work out most difficulties—if both people wanted to succeed badly enough.

She shut the thoughts down. Where Chad was concerned, she couldn't quite make up her own mind. Although tonight she needn't make compromises, the evening wasn't just for pleasure. It was to see if they meshed, to see if being together was as good as she thought it might be.

The attendant smiled kindly at Brittany as she studied a black lacquer of mirrored art, her reflection staring back and depicted over and over to infinity. She couldn't tell where one image ended and the next began. She couldn't see her entire reflection, only bits and pieces that extended into the mirrored night.

"Your first visit to the Starlight Room?"

"My first visit to Eden." *Her first time with Chad.* The thought made a bevy of butterflies light in her stomach.

The attendant led her into a dual-purpose room. An enormous shower with multi-showerheads and etched glass doors stood in one corner. Along one wall, a makeup counter with a plush chair invited her to sit in front of the silver-laminated vanity with dozens of interesting containers lined up under a huge mirror.

"Freshly laundered clothing is over here." The attendant opened a sliding mirror to reveal a huge selection of designer gowns, shoes, teddies and robes in a variety of sizes. "Please help yourself. Remember, no one will disturb you until noon tomorrow." She walked over to a computer monitor and tapped the screen. "Food can be discreetly delivered. All you need do is order on the touch plate. A chime will notify you of the food's arrival. You pick up your meal at the Carry-Thru window. Dispose of the utensils in the same place.''

Food was the last thing on Brittany's mind. When the attendant left, she took a quick shower and then searched the closet for something exotic. She had no idea of Chad's tastes, but he was a man. All man.

What would he like? Perhaps a silver teddy with matching heels?

A pair of delicate silver panties caught her eye and then an idea came to her, an idea so bold that she went about putting it into action at once, humming a little under her breath to steady her nerves. She spotted what she needed—silver body powder—on the counter. Opening the jar, she sniffed. At the scent of the sugary confection, she read the ingredients and learned the powder was sparkly under the black lights in the Starlight Room and, even better, was edible.

Brittany quickly stepped into the panties and then spread the rich, shimmering powder over her breasts, her tummy and down to her hips until it appeared she was wearing a silver swimsuit. Not enough. She coated her legs to her ankles, her arms to her wrists, leaving her face, hands, feet and back bare.

She turned in front of the mirror, admiring her handiwork. Although standing there nude except for heels and panties, she appeared to be wearing a sleek cat suit. In the dim lights of the room they would share, her flesh would sparkle under the black lights.

He wouldn't know she wasn't dressed until he touched her.

Quickly she twisted her hair up, smoothed silver sparkle gel into it for added flash and secured it with one silver hairpin. She already anticipated the moment when Chad would discover the secret of her outfit. Couldn't wait until he took out the pin and let her hair fall to her shoulders.

Taking a deep breath, she stepped through a door into the Starlight Room, wondering if Chad would already be there. He wasn't. But she gasped in pleasure. The black night sky overhead dominated the room, the stars shining brightly like tiny diamonds on black velvet. Black lighting made her every movement sparkle as she'd hoped, but it was the clouds suspended both high and low above a foggy floor that captured her attention.

The clouds swirled lazily at different levels. She approached one and understood they would serve as beds. Tiny microwires suspended them in the air as they circled the room slowly, dipping to the floor, then rising skyward.

Tilting her head back, she admired the observatory-like effect. At the highest part of the dome, a crescent moon spun, shooting shimmering moonlight below.

The man-made fog on the floor created an out-of-this-world setting and also sent a slight chill swirling about her legs. Then a door opened and she spied Chad.

He wore silk loungewear pants in a dark silver—and nothing else. His chest was bare, his dark hair wet and slicked back. And despite the exotic room, his hungry gaze focused only on her, heating her from across the room. "You look…like a midnight fantasy."

"You picked a terrific dream room."

"And a more terrific dream partner."

She thought of the sugar coating her body, and it turned her voice husky. "Wait until you taste me." Her feet, sure of themselves despite the fog and the heels, boldly strode over to him as if they were directing her brain and not the other way round.

She held her arms out wide. "What do you think?"

"That you smell like sugar. Good enough to eat."

While his response pleased her, she wanted to delay his discovery a little longer. "I meant, what do you think about the clouds?" She placed her palm on one of the lower moving ones and was surprised as her hand sank up to her elbow into a blanket of feathers with a satin coverlet. "I think this one is too soft."

Chad's fingers skimmed another cloud. "And this one's too hard." He pressed a button in the wall that she hadn't noticed until now.

At the hum of smooth machinery thrumming, she looked up. The crescent moon overhead was descending from the ceiling on more microwires. "The moon is a bed?"

A mattress had been cleverly crafted to fit inside the crescent moon.

"I believe it'll be just right."

When the moon reached the floor, the machinery

went silent. Chad gestured her to a set of steps. "Have you ever swung from a star?"

"Swung?"

Chad took her hand in his. "After we get in, the moon will take us back into the sky. You aren't afraid of heights, are you?"

"Course not." Still she hesitated. "The bed's going to swing while we…"

He lifted an eyebrow. "That's the idea."

"Suppose the power fails?"

"Then we'll be stuck up there. Together." Chad's sexy tone made her shiver, but she wasn't worried about a power blackout. Nor was she worried about being stuck up there without her clothes. It was that, for a moment, she'd taken a mental step back and realized just how much she wanted to be with Chad.

The thought didn't frighten her. Quite the contrary. Emboldened by her sense of rightness in the moment, she kicked off her shoes before stepping onto the stairs, then sat on the crescent moon's fitted mattress and slick satin sheets. Heated pillows lined a backrest that surrounded the bed, keeping the setting safe, plush and intimate.

Within moments Chad joined her and pressed a button that lifted them skyward. He sat beside her, close but not touching, monitoring their progress. Finally the magical ride stopped, leaving them suspended under the stars and surrounded by clouds. "Don't let me forget to thank your mother," he teased.

"Don't you dare!"

"Ashamed of wanting me?"

"On the contrary." She turned toward him, tilted her head and nibbled his ear. "Some things are private." She wasn't ready to admit to her mother how great she felt to be here. Here with Chad.

He retaliated for her ear nibble with a shoulder nip. He suddenly pulled back, his eyes wide with surprise as he licked his lip. "Are you wearing an edible bodysuit?"

"I hope you like sugar."

"I don't think I'll be able to get enough." He trailed a hand from her chin to her neck to her collarbone. "My God! You're naked."

"Except for my panties," she continued, enjoying the surprise on his face and the sparkle of pleasure in his eyes.

"I thought…"

"Yes?"

"That you should wear this sexy outfit in public."

"And now?"

"I want you to wear it only for me."

She leaned back on the bed, half sitting, arching her back so he would notice her breasts. "I can live with that—under one condition."

"What?" His gaze focused exactly where she wanted. On her taut nipples.

"I want your full attention."

"That can be arranged," he promised, his voice warm with desire. "But first, you have to promise not to move." He reached out one finger and touched the tip of her breast. "I like that pose. Too bad I don't have a camera."

"Take a mental picture."

"I have. You're a wanton-looking sight that I'll never forget. Not even in my dreams."

He inched closer but didn't touch her again. She ached to draw him closer. But he'd already taught her that waiting prolonged the pleasure. So she waited, wondering why this man could make her so hot with a nip and the briefest of touches when all others since her divorce had left her cold.

What was it about him that made her heartbeat thump out of control, that made her breath hitch in her throat, that made her willing to risk her heart for a night with him? She didn't know. Besides how could she think when he so clearly wanted to devour her?

She only knew that with him she felt confident, sexy. With him she could roll the dice and gamble on the future. This was a man she wanted to win.

Win?

As his head dipped and his tongue swirled around her nipple, her thoughts slipped away into a sea of sensation. She focused on a star glittering brightly overhead. "Have you ever wished upon a shining star?"

"Mmm." His tongue never stopped moving, and her every nerve ending flared with heat.

"You gave me three wishes at the masquerade. It's my turn to reciprocate. So what do *you* wish for?" she asked him. Since she'd promised not to move, she could only use words to distract herself from the intense pleasure before she found herself begging.

"Everything I want is right here," he murmured as he released one breast to capture the other.

"I'm serious."

"Uh-huh."

"You have no wishes?"

He licked his way up to her neck. "I want you to enjoy tonight as much as I will."

"That's all?"

"That's everything."

Before she could say another word, his mouth swooped down on hers. He tasted of powdered sugar and spiced wine. His muscled chest brushed against her breasts, and she longed to fling her arms around his neck, pull him closer.

But she'd given her word that she would hold this pose for him and felt wickedly decadent, sensuously female and intoxicated by his inventiveness. He kissed her expertly, leaving her breathless yet eager for more.

When he pulled back, she could see starlight reflected in his eyes. Eyes darkly mysterious with passion and glinting with a charming mischievousness. "Time for a new pose."

"You have a preference?" she asked. Stretching languidly, she knew his gaze would be drawn to her chest and hoped for more of his attention there. Her breasts, still silver with shimmer powder—except for her aroused, erect and very achingly hard nipples, which he'd sucked clean—needed more of his caresses.

"We should take full advantage of the view." He tilted his head to the side as if considering possibilities while she wanted to snap at him to hurry.

How could he remain this calm? She could clearly see his arousal beneath his silk loungewear, yet he appeared to be no more turned on than if out for an afternoon stroll. That was until his eyes locked with hers and his dilated pupils revealed his need.

"Where do you want me?" she asked, fully willing to let him make the decision. He might want a view. She wanted him.

One end of the bed tilted upward at an angle, forming a natural backrest. He patted it. "Scoot up here."

She did as he asked until she was half sitting, half reclining. He pulled out her hairpin and carefully fanned her hair across the pillow. Placed her hands at her sides. Then he hooked his fingers into her panties and tugged them off.

On her back, she had a magnificent view of the stars, but what held her gaze was him. Years of swimming and SEAL training had sculpted muscular arms and a wide chest, but it was the way he focused on her that made her squirm with pleasure. She was so lucky to have found a man with a slow hand and a gentle touch.

Her legs were straight but apparently not in the pose he preferred. He bracketed her ankles with his hands, and she thought he might part her thighs. He did.

But he also bent her legs so the pads of her feet rested on the cool satin sheet. She was totally open to his gaze, and he took a long, slow, appreciative look.

"Are you comfy?"

"Not exactly."

He moved her feet a tad wider. "Better?"

"Not exactly."

"What?"

"You *are* going to touch me, aren't you?"

"Oh, yeah."

"Soon?" She tried and failed to keep the pleading tone from her question.

"I have a few arrangements to make first."

She let out a groan, licked her lip and watched him snap out one of the cushions from the backrest. A compartment filled with all kinds of paraphernalia captured his attention.

"What's in there?" she asked warily, breasts aching, thighs already trembling for his expert caresses.

"Condoms."

"Oh." She hadn't thought that far ahead and chided herself. It wasn't like her to forget such important matters, but Chad had a way of making her head spin, her heart sputter and her body spasm with need.

Chad slipped off his silk pants, tore open a foil packet and chuckled.

"Oh, is right."

"Huh?"

"These are made specially for the Starlight Room."

As he rolled the condom over his sex, she gasped at the sudden color change. The condom was glow-in-the-dark metallic silver.

Corners of his eyes crinkling with amusement, he kneeled between her parted knees. "This will certainly be a night to remember."

"In more ways than one, I hope."

"Definitely." He skimmed his fingers along the insides of her knees, creating an answering tingle between her thighs.

"So do something already," she demanded.

"I haven't finished my very tempting dessert."

He'd left no doubt that he considered her the dessert as, with a lap of his tongue, he suckled her knee gently. She suddenly realized she'd made a very large mistake. The man had a sweet tooth all right, and she suspected he intended to sip up every sugary morsel from her flesh before making love to her.

Her anticipation warred with her impatience as he licked off the sugar until she could barely keep from squirming. Holding still forced her to focus on every stroke of his tongue along her thigh, every caress of his hands on her hips, every puff of his breath on her skin.

"Chad?"

"Mmm."

"Could you hurry?"

"Sure, babe."

He agreed easily but didn't increase his speed so

much as one nanosecond. He lingered between her upper thighs, and tiny groans came from the back of her throat.

Lightly he cupped her sex. "Ready for a new pose?"

"Only if you promise to make love to me."

"I promise."

He placed her calves on his shoulders so she was open and ready for him. He scooted forward, sitting on his heels, knees spread, his thighs bracketing her bottom and hips. Leaning over her, he once again took her breast into his mouth and she let out a soft sigh of encouragement. Simultaneously his fingers dipped between her legs, finding the moisture between her thighs.

He was taking her exactly where she wanted to go—on a midnight fantasy she'd never forget. His fingers worked in delicate, taunting circles that matched the rhythm of his tongue. Deep inside, pressure built, escalating until she knew one more touch would bring on the release she sought.

And that was when he stopped.

"Chad, I'm so…close."

"I know."

"I want you…inside me."

"That's where I want to be, too."

She angled herself toward his straining sex, but couldn't position herself to accomplish her wish. "Chad, if you don't enter me now…I'll—"

"You'll what?" He rubbed the tip of his hardness

teasingly, not entering her, lingering at the threshold of the ache he'd so expertly created.

"How can I think when you—" She gasped in delight as he plunged his sex into her in one deep, hard thrust.

Then he held perfectly still.

She started to pump her hips, recalled that he'd asked her not to move and realized that he'd found a new way to spike the growing tension inside her. Biting her lower lip, she vowed not to speak or she would be hearing herself beg. She bit harder especially when his fingers again teased her soft folds, taking her up, higher and higher, until her mind was as fuzzy as the clouds and as nebulous as the stars.

She was going to burst like a shooting star.

But he withdrew his hand.

Missing his heat, she opened her eyes to discover him leaning over her, his eyes dark, shadowed, passionate. His hands grasped the side of the bed, his teeth bit lightly on her nipple and then as he flexed his arms and legs, the bed began to sway.

Above her head, stars coalesced in the sky. The sensation inside her, the ebb and surge of him as the bed swung across the heavens was unlike anything she'd ever felt. He thrust his hips, driving, slowly, ever so slowly, timing his loving to coincide with the swinging crescent moon bed.

Blood rushed to her head, her fingers, her toes. Every part of her concentrated on the hub of her pleasure. He rocked in and out, and she lost all notion of time and place.

There was only Chad. And her.

She followed the rhythm, her senses flaring with a passion that had her wrapping her legs and feet around his hips, her fingers digging into his back to draw him closer. All the while he kept moving, kept swinging the bed, and then he was reaching between her legs, taking her higher.

"Come with me, babe." He found her lips. "Come with me to the stars."

Like exploding fireworks, they set each other into a frenzy, bursting in a starburst of lusty red haze. He gasped in release, then held her tightly.

Five minutes later she was still seeing stars all right, still trying to recover from her racing heart and the most powerful orgasm she'd ever had. For a moment, she'd seen stars burning and bursting behind her eyes as the pleasure spread from deep in her core to capture every part of her body and mind.

Like a too-bright light had shone in her eyes, she needed time to recover from the blinding sensations. Her limbs still quivered from the aftereffects and her thoughts whirled in a thousand directions.

She held tight to Chad, waiting for her lungs to draw in enough oxygen to clear her head. It took some time, not that she was in any hurry. She enjoyed the feel of Chad's chest against hers. Liked the rasp of his breath by her ear. Appreciated that he hadn't withdrawn his body from hers but held her tenderly.

Finally her thoughts cleared, leaving her in emotional turmoil. Because suddenly her feelings for this man were clear.

She loved him.

And she hadn't the faintest idea what to do next.

# *12*

IN THE LATE MORNING hours after their night of wild lovemaking, Chad remained wide-awake, holding Brittany in his arms, content to watch her sleep. Time after time, she'd surprised him with both her bold and brazen moves and her sheer joy at the numerous ways they'd relished, ravished, each other's bodies. Without a doubt, she had not one flake of glimmer powder left on her magnificent body. She had been one sweet treat for his hungry taste buds, one fine meal for his empty heart.

He'd never been with a woman who could give and take as much as she. Not even in his boyhood fantasies had he dreamed up a night like that one. In reality they'd reached an almost surreal state of perfection. Her wondrous capacity had kept up with his own appetites. Her emotions seemed to mirror his.

He'd probably let thoughts of Brittany distract him from his mission. Yet he had no regrets and would look back fondly on their time together—probably when he was sweating in some desert hellhole or freezing in the North Sea and cursing himself for being a fool and letting the best thing to happen to him in years slip away.

With her lips slightly swollen from his kisses, faint circles under her eyes from their all-nighter, she needed sleep. Yet he couldn't help his yearning to wake her again. To watch her eyes go from sleepy with passion to ragged with need. To hear soft moans of pleasure turn to a sensual scream.

She let out a soft sigh and curled into his body heat, nestling against his side so they fit like two well-matched puzzle pieces. He wondered if he could extend their time together past his mission's completion, past his leave. Would she want to continue their relationship in the outside world when she knew he could pick up and leave on a moment's notice and be gone for weeks on end?

So many questions. He had to put them aside. Concentrate on finding Lyle.

They hadn't stopped their lovemaking last night to eat, and his rumbling stomach reminded him that it required food after strenuous exercise. They both needed to leave enough preparation time so he could be watching the Fetish Room to see which couple had rented it for the night.

Chad awakened Brittany with a kiss, and after eating a magnificent breakfast, taking a shower and getting dressed, they exited the Starlight Room. Her skin glowed and satisfaction warmed him that he'd help put back the bounce in her step, reawakened the sparkle in her hazel eyes and established a rapport that had them comfortable together, even in silence as they strolled between the public buildings.

Eventually they settled onto a well-placed wrought-iron bench. In daylight, the entertainment district looked more magnificent than the night before. Wide, clean sidewalks wound between fountains, hedges and rosebushes. Parked golf carts testified to the rooms still occupied. Many couples walked arm in arm, and he hoped that whoever had rented the Fetish Room hadn't left early, since it was one of his few leads to finding Lyle. Occasionally he saw a three-some or someone who looked as if he'd partied too hard, but he never saw Lyle.

Beside him, Brittany suddenly elbowed his rib. The doorway of the Fetish Room had just opened and a couple emerged. A short Hispanic woman and her Latin lover. Chad had suspected finding Lyle might not be so easy, but disappointment still tugged at him. He'd been hoping to complete his mission quickly so he could devote the rest of his time here exclusively to Brittany. "It's not him."

"I guess we'll have to come back." Brittany delicately smacked her lips. "I've a mind to try the Island Room and…" Her words trailed off and an odd look crossed her features.

He turned around to see what had stopped her mid-sentence. "What?"

"I saw Mother walk out from between two buildings."

"So?"

"She was alone."

He heard concern and puzzlement in her tone, but as the rooms emptied, he kept scanning the growing throng. "Maybe Samantha was making a reservation for tonight or checking out a room in advance."

"But she hasn't made any effort to meet anyone," she protested. "I don't get it. Why would she come to Eden if she's determined to remain alone?"

Chad was about to give her a reassuring answer when a tall, blond man caught his attention. "Look at that guy over there."

"Where?"

Chad stood, grabbed her hand and yanked her to her feet. "It's Lyle."

THE TALL BLOND MAN HADN'T spotted Chad. Threading their way through the couples exiting the private rooms, Chad made sure he and Brittany kept at a distance from Lyle. Beside him, Brittany tried to hurry him along. "Don't you want to talk to him?"

"Eventually."

"Why not now?"

He couldn't help smiling at her impatience. "I want to see where he goes."

"So that if he gives us the slip, you can find him again?"

"Yeah." Chad thought back to when he'd spied his quarry. He'd seemingly appeared out of nowhere. Chad hadn't seen him exit any of the rooms. "If I hadn't been watching carefully, I might have thought he'd exited the Fetish Room, but he didn't."

"Maybe he was walking down the sidewalk and you didn't notice him until then."

"He's almost as tall as me," Chad pointed out with a frown.

"Kind of hard to miss," she agreed. "Where do you think he's going?"

"To take a woman to his hideout, I hope."

"That's because you're such a romantic."

"I can't believe it's taken so long to find him."

"You've been here less than a week." Brittany shot him a sideways glance, her eyes slit with suspicion. "You make it sound as if the hours crawled like months."

He squeezed her hand. "Nothing of the sort. I wanted to finish the mission so I could concentrate all my time on you."

Her frown disappeared. "I like the sound of that."

"Thought you would." Chad slowed their pace as Lyle entered a store. Eden didn't have many. The wide variety of merchandise reminded Chad of the general mercantile stores in small third-world countries that carried food, hardware and clothing. Except as they entered this store, he could see the goods were top-of-the-line, the lighting excellent and the service enthusiastic.

A saleswoman approached them as they tailed Lyle from the grocery department through the pharmacy. "May I help you?"

"We're browsing, thank you," Brittany said, sending her on her way. "When are you going to talk to him?" she asked quietly.

"Not yet," Chad replied, hoping his plan wouldn't go too far awry. He hadn't thought too carefully about his first meeting with Lyle since he couldn't know when or where it would happen. He only knew he didn't want to approach in a situation where Lyle could easily flee. Chad recalled how the other man had all too easily eluded him the night of the masquerade. Right now, this was Lyle's home ground. Chad was the intruder.

"He's stopping in that aisle, picking up a tube of caulking, or maybe paint," Brittany said. "What do you want to do?"

"I need to keep him in sight. Pretend you're interested in something."

"Edible underwear?" Brittany picked up a package and kept a straight face. "Do you prefer cherry or apricot?"

Chad chuckled softly. "I have a voracious appetite, as you know. We can buy both, but not now. I don't want to get held up at a checkout counter and lose track of him."

"Now this is interesting." Brittany picked up an item.

"What?" He didn't pay much attention as Lyle picked up a toothpaste tube and read the label.

"Erotic oil. It heats the skin when you blow on it."

"Is it edible?"

"You have a one-track mind."

"I'll take that as a compliment." He grabbed Brittany's hand. "Let's go. He's on the move."

They followed Lyle directly to the checkout counter, where he purchased the tube. Hidden by stacks of perfume, Chad peered around the corner for his first up-close look. Definitely Lyle Gates. His hair might be a tad blonder and three inches longer, his face might look more tanned and relaxed than Chad remembered, but this was definitely Admiral Gates's son.

He leaned and whispered into Brittany's ear. "If he does spot us and take off, I may have to leave you behind. In that contingency, I'll meet you back at the house when I can."

"I'm a pretty good runner."

"With your long legs I don't doubt it. But after last night, you might not be up for a five-mile run."

She grinned. "You won't lose me easily. I'm in good shape."

"Excellent shape. I especially like how your breasts fit in my hands."

He liked it when she blushed but didn't have time to keep baiting her. "He's leaving."

They headed out the door, giving Lyle an ample head start. He turned back the way he'd come and Chad wondered if he could have a love nest somewhere in the entertainment area. "Are there any private lodgings among the public rooms?"

"I don't know."

They strolled past a dwindling number of couples. Most of the crowd from the private rooms had vacated and gone to other areas. With the thinning crowds, there was a greater risk of being spotted, so Chad increased the distance between them.

Lyle had walked past the Bondage Room and toward the Fetish Room when he suddenly disappeared.

Brittany looked at Chad, her hazel eyes dark with confusion. "Where did he go?"

The man seemed to appear and disappear out of thin air. Chad knew damn well he was no magician. He recalled teaching Lyle hand-to-hand combat and knew the man was real flesh and blood.

"Maybe he works in one of the rooms as an attendant," Brittany said, trying to help. "I've heard of men who weren't popular finding other work in Eden. It's very lucrative."

"There's only one problem with your theory. Lyle was in demand. Laurel wanted him. He had something going with Aurora, too."

"We know Lyle had a thing for her. We have no idea if she ever purchased his services." Brittany sounded skeptical.

If he thought they might be walking into danger, he would have sent her away, but Lyle wasn't a violent sort. In fact, Chad had had to work hard to bring out the man's survival instincts. Lyle had tended to fight by the rules, passed his SEAL training, kept to himself. As a result, Chad hadn't known him well.

They approached the entrance to the Fetish Room, and Chad searched for a place where Lyle could have disappeared. A drain pipe. A rooftop. A hidden doorway.

The concrete wall curved slightly and suddenly the sidewalk curved around what seemed to be a private lane. Flowering plants in baskets hung over the narrow path that ended at a front doorway of gorgeous stained glass in hues of gold and emerald.

As they neared, Chad increased their pace. Next to the door was a doorbell.

"Now what?" Brittany asked.

Chad rang the bell.

# 13
_____

BRITTANY JUMPED in surprise when a blond man answered the door. She'd expected more drama. Perhaps Chad picking the lock or climbing through a window.

Lyle Gates was tall, rather broad shouldered, with bottle-green eyes. His hair cascaded over one eye, and he shook it back impatiently, revealing the hint of a half defiant, half remorseful expression on his intelligent face. In his late twenties to early thirties, he was in the process of tying on a khaki smock with dark smudges on it over tight-fitting jeans and a T-shirt. He wiped rough, chapped hands with strong, tapered fingers over the smock, before offering Chad his hand.

"I've been expecting you," Lyle admitted to Chad. "I've had a few days to prepare since I eluded you at the masquerade."

"So that _was_ you," Chad murmured as Lyle turned to her.

He shook her hand, too. "You must be Brittany."

"How'd you know?" she asked.

Lyle ignored her question, instead leading them into his home. Sketches dominated the walls of the living area that had been cleared of furniture. Clean lines, sharp proportions and a gentle balance showed the artist's keen eye for detail in the women's bodies he seemed to favor. Most of the women's faces didn't show enough to reveal their identities, but Lyle seemed partial to one woman whom he'd sketched repeatedly. Brittany leaned over a counter to look at an easel and knocked a book onto the floor. Stooping to pick it up, she dislodged a paper—a letter that started, "Darling, I love you."

Brittany replaced the private note inside the book and examined more sketches, but her mind was no longer on Lyle's art. Who had written that letter and how long ago had those words been written? Was Lyle still in love? Was it this woman who had been hiding him?

The tube of hardener they'd seen him buy in the store sat unopened on the counter next to a still-wet clay sculpture. Lyle moved as eagerly to the piece as a treasure hunter to a glint of gold. "Would you mind if I work while we talk?"

"It's your place." Chad straddled another stool. "I'm sure you can guess that the admiral sent me."

Brittany strolled around the room, admiring the sketches. Most of the women she didn't recognize. There was one of Laurel, not particularly flattering; yet with the cigar clamped between her teeth and the rhinestones glinting, he'd captured her perfectly, contrasting the impudence and intelligence of a youthful spirit with the encroaching age and relentless battle against her infirmity in her wheelchair. There was one of Aurora, all eyes and hair. She seemed somehow bolder on paper than in real life—as if the artist had seen not only who she was but the woman she could become. The majority of women remained faceless, yet from the style, Brittany could tell he'd drawn the same mystery woman over and over and she wondered if this might be his lover.

"The admiral sent you to convince me to come back?" Lyle's strong fingers smoothed the clay, his fingers sure and accurate, forming shoulders and a foundation on which to create a woman's head.

"Yes." Chad answered simply.

"He knows I'm here."

"He said you were due home months ago."

"I told him I'd extended my contract."

"He didn't say that to me." Chad frowned. "In fact, he told me he was worried that you might be held here against your will."

Lyle kept working, but Brittany could hear the frustration in his tone. "Dad knows I'm here. He knows I'm safe and happily working on my art." He looked up and pierced Chad with a glare. "I don't enjoy being sent to godforsaken, third-world rock piles where I might get shot. The admiral knows I don't want to be a SEAL anymore."

"Then why did he send me here?" Chad asked reasonably.

Although Brittany took her time perusing the sketches on the walls, she couldn't help noticing Chad's casual tone, as if he couldn't quite believe the admiral had lied to him. Lyle attempted to match his informal demeanor, but the man's gifted hands gave him away. He spoke about the admiral, and his smooth strokes became short and choppy.

"Dad knows you're the most gung-ho SEAL there is and if anyone could talk me into re-upping it's you. We've had many conversations about my career. In the end, it's my choice, my decision."

"Can't argue with you there. He's worried about you, and this sure puts me in one hell of a spot."

Chad spoke gently enough, but there was a hint of steel behind his even tone. Brittany suspected he didn't know whether to believe Lyle or the admiral, but Chad had found Lyle to be in Eden under his own volition. The facts made the admiral out to be the one who'd distorted the truth. Apparently the man wouldn't be satisfied unless his son followed in his footsteps.

At least Samantha had never pressured Brittany to model for high-fashion designers like her mother. She had never even suggested that Brittany join the cosmetics empire she'd built. Instead, she'd encouraged her daughter to find her own way.

Then Brittany had made a mess of her life by marrying Devlin. She thought back and Brittany realized that Samantha had never criticized her for loving such an unfaithful man. She'd only offered support, even moving out of her house and staying elsewhere in Eden to give Brittany privacy. Brittany may not have had a father, but she'd hit the jackpot with Samantha for a mother.

Chad leaned forward, his eyes intent. "The admiral's my boss. If I don't bring you back, he might station me in Timbuktu for the rest of my hitch.''

"I served my time in the military," Lyle countered, using logic to argue each point. "I have an honorable discharge. No way will I re-up.''

Chad shrugged. "Then I guess we're at an impasse.''

Lyle met Chad's gaze squarely.

"I'll tell you what. How about a little bet on a wrestling contest? Whoever scores the first pin wins.''

"If I win?" Chad asked.

"I'll leave Eden and go back to Dad long enough to talk to him in person and demand he get off my back. If I win," Lyle continued, "you go away and leave me alone.''

Brittany rolled her eyes at the ceiling. Men and their testosterone. Could they settle this by compromise or reasoning? No. They had to resort to a barbaric wrestling match.

Lyle's tone was firm as he untied his smock. "I won't make it easy on you.''

"I didn't expect you would. Weren't you All-American in college?''

Lyle eyes glinted with challenge. "So?''

Chad seemed more amused than perturbed, as if talking through their differences was out of the question. "There's more of the admiral in you than you think.''

"We're both stubborn.''

"All men are stubborn," Brittany interrupted. "Can't you compromise and talk this out? Lyle, why don't you just call your father so he knows you're okay and explain that you're set on staying here.''

"It won't do any good,'' both men said simultaneously as they turned to look at her. Chad restrained a tight smile.

Lyle shook his head. "Besides wrestling's more fun than talking.''

"Fun? You could both break something—though I doubt it would be anything unimportant like your heads.''

Lyle cleaned his hands on a towel. "One quick pin and then he'll leave me alone. If I win, I won't have to depart and disappoint…''

His voice softened and Brittany knew the ex-SEAL was in love. Again she wondered who the lady was.

Brittany took Chad's hand. "Could we talk about this…alone?''

Chad shook his head. "How about after we wrestle?''

Brittany let out a long, frustrated sigh. "Lyle, tell him you won't leave until he returns. Give him your word.''

Lyle's eyebrows rose as if he'd never consider running from a challenge. "Fine.''

Brittany dragged Chad out the front door before the two men began their ridiculous wrestling contest. She should have been surprised how easily Chad had given in to her wishes, but she was marshalling her arguments to talk him out of this fight. She didn't care how good at martial arts Chad was—if Lyle had wrestled in college, Chad could get his neck broken.

The minute the front door closed behind them, Chad spun her around and kissed her hard. He stole her breath and her thoughts spun in cartwheels. How did a woman deal with a man who wouldn't even let her speak? How could she convince him he was making a big mistake when he kept her breathless? Especially when under the urgency of his kiss was a tenderness that made her legs turn to jelly. If Chad was badly hurt, he'd end up in the hospital. She cared about his welfare, and she also cared that they might not ever finish what had started between them. She'd spend the rest of her life regretting that she hadn't even told him how she felt.

She pulled away with a gasp for air, ignoring the urge to draw him back against her, ignoring the urge to run her fingers through his hair and hold him close. Instead she let her underlying anger surface.

"You have no business wrestling with Lyle."

Chad stiffened. "I'm sorry you see it that way. Your leaving now is for the best. I want you safely away so I'm not distracted."

She used his patronizing tone to bolster knees still weak from his kiss. Releasing her temper, she let it soar free. "You big stubborn lughead. There needn't be any bet. Walk away."

Chad advanced. "No."

She retreated a step. Not that she was afraid of him, but she didn't want his hands on her, muddling her thinking. "He's a grown man. And he's in love."

"He didn't say that."

"He didn't have to. If you used your eyes, you

could see that he's staying here because of a woman."

Chad backed her up until her rear hit the wall. He planted a palm on either side of her shoulders, his powerful arms blocking her escape, but she didn't want to flee. She wanted to fight to keep him safe. Unfortunately, the banked fires in his eyes told her he didn't intend to give in to her.

He spoke softly, his voice all the more dangerous as it hardened with determination. "Exactly how do you know the man's in love?"

"Because I can hear it in his tone. See it in his eyes."

"You don't have a single fact to back up your opinion."

"I saw all those drawings of a special woman. And a love letter." She ignored his skepticism. "Maybe I'm sensitive to his feelings because I'm in love, too."

"That's the most ridiculous, illogical, stupid...did you say you're in love?" Chad's eyes narrowed to slits. A muscle throbbed in his cheek.

She hadn't meant to reveal her feelings, especially during a heated quarrel. "If you weren't so dense, I wouldn't have to repeat myself."

Chad shook his head as if to clear his mind of impossible thoughts. "Who are you in love with?"

"My pet rock...who obviously has more sensitivity than you."

"You can't just ambush me and expect me to know what to say."

"I know you're a guy, but that's no excuse."

"I don't know what to say."

"That's the problem, isn't it?"

Lyle stepped through the doorway into the alley, interrupting their quarrel. "When a woman tells a man she loves him, he isn't supposed to argue with her." He'd obviously been listening.

"Now you're the expert?" Chad asked. "During SEAL training, we had to drag you to meet ladies."

"Like a bar is a good place to meet the love of your life?"

"It's a start. As I recall, you weren't interested."

Brittany refused to look at Chad. She'd as good as told him she'd loved him and all he could do was chastise Lyle. She ignored the hurt building inside her chest, ignored her dashed hopes, ignored her disappointment. "Chad, this is no way to settle things. You could get hurt."

"I'm going to win."

"But—"

Lyle didn't take his gaze off Chad, but he spoke to Brittany. "It's time for you to leave."

"So you can kill each other in this alley? Why don't you go to a gym where there are nice soft mats?"

Chad rolled up his sleeves and turned to face Lyle. "This will be more interesting."

"You ready?" Lyle asked.

"Go," Chad ordered her.

Angry at being dismissed, fearful he'd have his brains bashed in, Brittany shrugged and backed off, but she had no intention of leaving the two of them alone. She'd seen wrestling on television where men pounded one another with body blows that could do major damage. Almost having reached the end of the alley, she turned around to watch.

In a crouch, the ex-SEAL approached Chad from his right. He lunged, shooting to grab Chad's knees. Chad shifted to the side—but not enough. Both men crashed to the pavement.

Brittany shuddered and moved closer, fascinated and horrified. She intended to stay out of Chad's way. Call for help if necessary. But then the two men scrambled to regain their feet and circled while she stood rooted to the spot, her mouth dry as dust. Whenever she saw a movie, two men fighting as a woman stood by and screamed, she always silently urged the woman to help her man, maybe grab a weapon or distract his opponent, or throw in a kick or elbow.

But these two men, physically so evenly matched, could accidentally swat her into the building like a fly. Before she could decide whether to try to help, Chad feinted to his left, lunged to his right and swept Lyle's feet out from under him.

The men rolled. Lyle ended up on top, then she heard Chad grunt, and she saw he'd extended Lyle's arm, pressing unnaturally and what must have been painfully against the elbow joint.

"Give up?" Chad asked, and Brittany held her breath, hoping they were done with their nonsense.

"No way, sailor. You've got me in an arm bar. We agreed on a pin."

Chad rolled free and both men stood breathing normally as if they'd exerted little effort. Lyle crouched down, and she realized they'd stopped and restarted the fight as if they had a referee sending them back to their respective corners.

Chad didn't look like a wrestler and didn't stand in Lyle's low crouch, nor did he advance like a boxer, or one of those kung-fu fighters. Instead he moved with the grace of a dancer, keeping his weight on the balls of his feet, elbows close to his body, maintaining total concentration. Lyle kept his center of gravity lower, only he didn't have Chad's speed or lightness of movement.

"Ready for round two?" Chad asked the other man.

"No more fancy-shmancy tricks."

Brittany racked her brain, trying and failing to come up with a solution that Chad and Lyle would both accept.

"This is no way to settle—" she began,

"Get out of here," Chad barked at her.

"I won't let him hurt you," she argued back. Although Chad had caught the other man in an arm bar, wrestling was clearly Lyle's preferred mode of fighting. Yet Chad didn't seem the least bit worried. In fact, he appeared to be enjoying himself.

Chad circled to the right. "He won't hurt me. However, I do appreciate your vote of confidence." He spoke sarcastically and conversationally to Brittany while both men looked for an opening or weakness.

Chad evaded Lyle's advance, but barely, breaking

the other man's grappling hold and smoothly shifting forward. Lyle's efforts were more of a scramble, and he was breathing heavily now, as if he hadn't kept in shape. Chad still hadn't broken a sweat. Not even a hair out of place, he looked as if he'd just stepped out and returned with the morning newspaper.

She sensed it was only a matter of time until either Chad made a mistake or Lyle wore down. Apparently Chad realized his opponent was tiring, too. Chad maintained a defensive stance, ready to deflect a major move, but not on the attack.

Lyle spoke softly, sweat trickling down his brow. "I'm going to take you down soon."

Chad didn't flinch. "Dream on."

While Brittany listened to the men taunt each other, Samantha appeared out of nowhere, although she must have come up behind Brittany from the main street. Her mother walked down the sidewalk, straight toward the men and scolded Chad. "You better not hurt Lyle."

"Mother!" What was she doing here?

Samantha, looking buff and polished as usual in a black miniskirt, cream blouse and her hair loose and flowing, gave the appearance of a woman a decade younger. Moving with her normal take-control attitude, she joined Brittany and frowned at the men.

"Why are they fighting?" her mother asked, as the men flexed muscles, grabbed for leverage and rolled, each trying to gain the advantage.

Brittany shrugged. "A stupid bet. They're as stubborn as you are. I thought maybe if they knocked their heads together it would beat some sense into them.''

''We couldn't get that lucky.''

''We?'' As compelling as the fight going on before her eyes was, Brittany knew she was missing something. ''What are you doing here? Were you following me?''

Samantha chuckled, drawing a frown from Brittany.

Before she could ask Samantha another question, the two men regained their footing.

Chad lunged, his movements blurry-fast. With a grunt and twist, he pinned Lyle to the ground. Immediately Chad stood, offered his hand to Lyle and helped him to his feet. ''Looks like you're going back to—''

''I changed my mind.'' Lyle reached into his pocket, pulled out a Taser, yanked Samantha against him and aimed the weapon against her neck. ''I'm not going anywhere.''

# 14

CHAD HELD OUT HIS HANDS in an unthreatening manner, aware that this narrow corridor had no security cameras. He should have taken Lyle down with a disabling blow when he had the opportunity. The problem was he'd trusted the man to abide by certain unspoken gentlemanly rules. Chad had taught him the basics of hand-to-hand combat and had known him to be a man of his word. Chad had misjudged Lyle. As long as the ex-SEAL aimed the weapon in Samantha's direction, he couldn't risk a bold maneuver.

If only Brittany had left when he'd told her to. Now she could be in danger, too. Unfortunately, the woman who'd called him stubborn seemed to share that trait. Why had she stayed? He supposed he shouldn't have expected her to take his orders without question like a member of Red Squad. Still, if she'd listened, he'd have one less thing to worry about.

He was worried. Lyle was not the same man he remembered. He seemed more determined. More mature and just as smart as ever, Lyle had made Chad doubt the admiral's story. Lyle's offer to return to square things with the admiral would have taken Chad off the hook, so he'd accepted the bet.

But what the hell was Samantha doing here? Was it a coincidence she'd stopped by? He thought not. Was she looking for Brittany? Or was there something else he was missing?

While he didn't believe Lyle would stun Samantha, even though he held the Taser to her throat, Chad wouldn't take any chances. The shock might not do any permanent damage, but it still hurt.

"Lyle, let me go," Samantha demanded with the imperious command of a woman who expects to be obeyed. She didn't look the least bit frightened. In fact her eyes sparkled with what he thought might be amusement. He had to be mistaken. People reacted to danger and stress differently, but there was nothing amusing about Lyle threatening Samantha.

Lyle motioned Brittany to join Chad, without releasing Samantha. "Do as I say and no one will be hurt."

Samantha sighed. "I should hope not."

"Do as he says, Mother." Brittany joined Chad and he felt better with his arm around her. If he got the chance, he'd shove her to safety.

Lyle spoke quietly but firmly. "I want you two to stroll over to the Bondage Room. Chad, book the place for the night, then we'll all have a little talk."

Chad shook his head. "Why don't we—"

"Now!" He lifted Samantha's chin slightly with the Taser, reminding them who was in charge, then he placed the Taser against her side, hiding the weapon from passersby.

"Fine," Brittany muttered, yanking Chad back to

the main street, with Lyle and Samantha following. "I always wanted to see the Bondage Room."

"You did?" he asked, making conversation, trying to think how to safely separate Samantha from the weapon at her side. Lyle had the advantage. He knew Chad's skill and kept far enough back to prevent him from trying a spinning back kick.

While Lyle wasn't a violent man, and Chad didn't believe he would hurt an innocent woman, Chad couldn't take unnecessary chances. Out here on the sidewalk with people strolling by, unaware of the conflict, Lyle appeared to simply be holding Samantha close, but the weapon in her side was a threat Chad wouldn't forget.

Chad spoke over his shoulder. "Look, let the women go and I'll—"

"Shut up." Lyle ordered. "Book the room. Then we'll talk."

"Bondage Room for four, coming right up." Chad used the computer terminal on the street. People passed by talking and eating, totally oblivious to the Taser hidden against Samantha's waist.

When attendants greeted them inside the Bondage Room doorway, Lyle motioned them back. "We'd like total privacy, please."

Brittany and Chad led the way through a changing room with the requisite closet of clothes and private shower into the main room. Chad had expected another large dome, but this was a warren of smaller rooms decorated like a space dungeon with all the modern trappings. They passed by a cozy emerald-

and-bronze room with a mirrored ceiling, a four-poster bed in dark green lacquer, and complimentary velvet handcuffs for feet and hands. Whips, chains and masks decorated the walls—all in shimmering silver. He saw a blue-carpeted room with only a cage that hung from the ceiling and a wall with straps to hold a person upright and a television screen on the far wall.

"To the right," Lyle ordered.

This room possessed one golden post that rose ten feet up from where it was set in the concrete floor. Padded gold leather wrapped the post like skin. Padded straps on the post and others set in the floor to bind the wrists and ankles would hold even Hercules motionless.

"Brittany, tie the man up."

"Is this really necessary?" Samantha asked, partially amused, partially dismayed.

"I'm not taking any chances."

"He didn't hurt you," Brittany defended Chad to Lyle, and Chad wondered if she realized that her mother was now a hostage because he hadn't wanted to take Lyle out with a disabling blow.

Lyle shook his head. "You don't know what he's capable of. I once saw him take down five armed men with his bare—"

"That's classified," Chad interrupted.

"So how come you survived your fight, if he's that good?"

"Tie him up and I'll explain, ladies. You have to understand, if he'd wanted to take me out, I would be down. I'm only standing here now because he played by the rules. He has the skill and confidence to defeat me without causing permanent damage. Your interference and the Taser saved me. So immobilize him, then we'll talk some more.''

"What if I say no?" Chad asked.

"I'll stun your girlfriend or her mother, I don't care which.''

"Lyle!" Samantha would have said more, but Lyle placed his palm over her mouth.

"Quiet.''

Chad walked to the post, turned around and slipped his hands into the cuffs.

No way could Brittany tighten the cuffs since his arms were over his head, and she wasn't tall enough to reach. Lyle would have to do it. When he approached, Chad could use his deadly feet to—

"Brittany, climb on the stool," Lyle directed.

Chad's hope of fighting his way free sank like a leaky ship headed for the ocean's bottom. With an apologetic look, she did as Lyle asked, shoving a golden stool in front of him.

"Pull the cuffs tight," Lyle directed.

She climbed onto the stool and adjusted the cuffs.

"Tighter," Lyle demanded.

As Brittany obeyed, his back flattened against the pliant leather. He tested the thick binding around his wrists and found no give, no weakness. He was in no physical pain and reminded himself he'd escaped from much worse positions.

His main concern was for the women. Lyle couldn't allow them to go free for fear they'd alert the authorities. Would he tie up the women, too? Maybe he wanted a head start to hide again.

"Lyle—"

"Quiet." Lyle motioned Brittany to tie the ankle straps.

Chad spread his feet and allowed her to restrain his ankles with the thick leather that ended in a taut chain connected to concrete, covered with plush golden carpet to hide the heavy-duty construction. Chad speared Lyle with a lift of his brow. "You feel safe enough to talk now?"

"I don't think you understand what's going on," Lyle said softly as he pocketed the Taser.

"Why don't you explain?" Brittany asked.

Samantha walked toward Brittany, her eyes cautious. "I should have told you sooner. I didn't think Chad would find Lyle and…"

"You knew I was looking for him?" Chad asked with a frown in her direction.

"That's why I changed the medical file," Samantha admitted. "I thought you'd give up if you thought he was dead."

"I knew you wouldn't give up until you found me, but she wouldn't listen," Lyle added.

"Mother, why would you go to the extreme of altering a medical file to protect Lyle? For that matter, how did you know Chad was even looking for him?"

"Because Lyle told me," her mother confessed.

A shocked look darkened Brittany's eyes. "*Lyle* told you?"

"You see, I'm the one who bought his contract."

*Lyle and Samantha?* Stunned, Chad couldn't believe he'd missed the connection and wondered if he'd been too wrapped up in his feelings for Brittany to put together the mystery. No wonder Brittany had never seen her mother with anyone else—her mother was already involved.

Chad watched Brittany absorb the shock and wished he could have been standing next to her to offer support. Her face paled beneath her tan, her eyes widened and, for once, she seemed unable to utter a word.

"Say something," Samantha pleaded.

"Give her a chance to absorb the surprise," Chad muttered, suddenly realizing he'd been taken for a fool. If Lyle and Samantha were an item, then Lyle would never have used the Taser on Samantha. The entire ruse had simply been to neutralize Chad. He called himself ten kinds of an idiot for falling for the trick. Lyle had been sly and clever, and it brought a smile to Chad's face since he couldn't help admiring the other man's audacity.

Brittany took her mother's hands between her own. "I don't know what to say. I can't believe you went to such extremes to hide your feelings for Lyle from me."

"After Jeffrey, I thought you'd disapprove, and I wanted to give us time to see where our feelings would lead. I figured there was no harm in keeping the secret, especially if things didn't work out."

"But they *have* worked out?" Brittany pressed, looking from her mother to Lyle and back.

"We aren't rushing into anything. For now we're happy together."

"What about Aurora?" Brittany was working through the details in a logical order, despite how shaken she obviously felt. "I thought Lyle climbed out of Laurel's window to go to her, not you."

"Aurora offered to give the impression that Lyle wanted her, so in case the admiral sent anyone looking for him, they wouldn't head straight to me…and find Lyle."

Brittany let out a long, low sigh. "I'm surprised. And hurt."

"Hurt?" Samantha asked. "I've been trying to protect you."

"From what? Didn't you trust me enough to understand? Don't you think I want you to be happy?"

Chad could hear the pain in Brittany's tone, but he also heard the underlying strength to accept whatever life or lover her mother chose for herself. The bond between these two women was strong and a little misunderstanding wouldn't break their relationship.

Her mother's voice was tight, strained. "I thought you had enough to deal with in your own life without Lyle and me complicating things."

"You aren't a complication, you're family." Brittany hugged Samantha, then pulled back, holding her mother's two hands.

Samantha's eyes teared. "After the mistake I made with Jeffrey, I didn't think you'd approve of another artist in my life. What's odd is that I believed Lyle was still a SEAL for months. He didn't tell me he'd left the navy or about his sculpting until later, and by then, I already knew he had an artist's soul, although I still think of him as a SEAL because he's so disciplined.''

Brittany looked from Lyle to Chad. "I do see the similarities. Both of them are fit, intelligent, kind and stubborn, not to be swayed from their goals. Didn't you realize that buying Chad for me would cause you difficulties?''

"Not at the time, I didn't. Besides your obvious attraction to Chad, I thought SEALs made excellent prospects. So after I hit it off with Lyle, I chose Chad for you, unaware of their former connection. At first I hid Lyle because I feared you'd worry about me, and I wanted you thinking about a man for yourself. When Lyle finally told me the likelihood that Chad was in Eden to search for him, it seemed easier to keep hiding him, but I never meant to shut you out.''

"I love you, Mother. If Lyle makes you happy, then I'll accept your decision. I won't hold his art against him because of Jeffrey." Tears brimmed in both their eyes. Mother, like daughter, refused to shed them.

"You don't mind that Lyle is—"

"My age?" Brittany shook her head. "You never did act your age, so I think you'll be perfect together. What I don't understand is why you told me that Chad was too young for you.''

"Another lie to throw you off track." Samantha let out a sigh. "Forgive me?"

"Of course."

"Now can someone please untie me?" Chad requested, knowing that he had a role to play here just as much as Brittany did with her mother. She'd recovered from the shock and reassured her mother, but she had to have a few doubts, ones she'd hidden well.

Samantha walked over to Chad but made no move to release his ankles or wrists. "Do you still intend to force Lyle to return to the admiral?"

Chad picked his words as carefully as if walking through a mine field. He had his own reasons for not yet divulging his change of mind. "Your contract with Lyle doesn't alter my obligations to the admiral."

"An unofficial mission," Brittany challenged him with a glint of mischievousness in her eyes.

Did she suspect he'd already decided to return to the admiral without Lyle? Nothing underhanded or illegal kept Lyle in Eden. There was no murder, not even a kidnapping. Only love for a woman. Despite Chad's loyalty to the admiral, he couldn't in good conscience kidnap the man because the admiral preferred that his son rejoin the navy to selling his services to a woman or enjoying his sculpting. Chad could take a little of the admiral's heat. Although his boss might be angry, Chad would find a way to calm him. For now he simply answered what Brittany asked.

"Unofficial is correct. However, I did give the admiral my word."

"And you gave me your word to stay in Eden until your contract is up."

"True."

Brittany circled him like a huntress on the scent of prey. "So, unless you intend to break your word to me, I have several weeks to change your mind."

Chad mentally applauded, unwilling to give an inch. "Sounds interesting."

Samantha chuckled. "Very interesting."

"Mother, you and Lyle should leave now."

Samantha shared an amused glance with Lyle. "You want us to help untie him?"

Chad held his breath, not quite daring to hope.

Brittany's eyes sparkled. "I think I'll save that pleasure for myself."

"Remember one thing," Lyle warned her. "You can hold a tiger by the tail but, eventually, you'll have to let him go."

"I'll take my chances," Brittany said softly, a provocative lilt in her words, as Lyle and Samantha departed arm in arm.

"You know you're beautiful when you take charge like that," Chad told her, for the first time allowing himself to dwell on the very pleasant memory of her telling him that she loved him. She'd caught him by surprise, something she was very good at and a trait he found extremely attractive.

"Compliments won't set you free."

*Good.* He didn't want her to turn him loose. Not

yet. He wanted to see how far Brittany would go. He recalled their first meeting when she'd frozen him with ice. Even then he'd sensed the passionate woman beneath the surface. He'd succeeded in coaxing out her true nature and suspected he was about to reap the benefits.

She had so much love to give, but did he want that love? Especially when he knew she'd be hurt after he returned to the outside world?

Would Chad destroy that love as he had his ex-wife's? Brittany had forgiven her mother's deception as easily as she reached up and unbuttoned his shirt, but she wouldn't let him off so simply. He hurt thinking about the pain he'd caused her when he hadn't responded to her assertion of love. He hadn't just been in denial about his own feelings, he hadn't had a clue what they really were.

Comfortable with her having the power to keep him restrained, he baited her. "What will set me free?"

"Me." She opened his shirt and ran the tip of one finger from throat to navel. "You'd look better naked."

"I'd like to oblige you but—"

She spun on her heel. "Don't go anywhere. I'll be right back."

For effect, he let out a low groan but was damn glad when she didn't look back to catch the hungry smile that had escaped him. He couldn't wait to see what she would do next.

BRITTANY PRACTICALLY SKIPPED her way back to the dressing room. She immediately buzzed the attendant and requested a pair of sharp shears that would cut material. Next, she stripped and ransacked the closet in pursuit of the perfect outfit. Black leather dominated the choices, and she spied what she wanted.

A slinky metallic gold minidress with a plunging neckline reminded her of chain mail. Nude, she slipped it over her head and admired herself in the mirror. The see-through material let the eyes play peek-a-boo with her bare flesh. She let down her hair, poured gold glitter into her hand, then liberally sprinkled it over her hair, face and shoulders.

She rummaged through the back of the closet and found knee-high boots and a belt with a scabbard. She didn't find a sword, so when the attendant returned with the shears, she placed the scissors inside.

Her hands shook a little at the brazen thoughts tumbling through her head. She recalled how Chad had teased and taunted her. Now it was her turn. Anticipation revved in her blood like a race car on the starting line.

It was payback time.

She intended to enjoy herself quite thoroughly. Enjoy Chad quite thoroughly. Along the way she hoped to convince the stubborn man she wouldn't wilt while he left on his SEAL missions.

She vowed Chad would change his mind. Oh yeah.

She just hoped, for both their sakes, he didn't change his mind too quickly.

# 15

CHAD EAGERLY WAITED for Brittany to return, wondering why she'd left and exactly how long it would take her to reappear, all the while tamping down his natural excitement. His martial arts training had given him extraordinary control over his body. He could make time pass faster for himself or even more slowly by employing yoga techniques. He could lower his pulse rate, control his breathing, even "switch off" his nerve receptors so his mind wouldn't recognize any pain his body endured.

Shutting off pain would also mean shutting off pleasure, which he wouldn't do. What about shutting down his emotions? Did he love her? Had he been denying his feelings? He didn't know. He only knew he didn't want to miss one moment of this exquisite time with Brittany.

She didn't disappoint him. His golden girl returned shortly, wearing a twenty-four carat smile and not much else. He couldn't count the scrap of material as a dress since the clingy silk hung so low on her chest that the shimmering cloth barely covered her hard and pink nipples.

At the sight of her, his mouth turned cottony dry. "Wow!"

She wore a belt at her waist and a long scabbard that lacked a sword. Her hair and shoulders glittered with golden sparkles that couldn't match the glint of desire in her eyes. A desire that equaled his still unnamed feelings.

Tossing aside a bag filled with clunky items, she approached him and pulled a pair of shears from her scabbard. "I want you naked."

He eyed the shears, noting that the lower blade had a flattened tip. The metal gleamed dangerously. He swallowed hard, but didn't protest as she knelt by his ankle and began to cut upward, biting his tongue rather than warning her to be careful.

With her head bent and her hair spilling over her shoulders, he couldn't quite see down her dress to distract himself from the cold metal snipping its way up his leg. She cut the material at his shin, his knee, his thigh, and as she straightened, he had a magnificent view down the front of her dress of firm, high breasts that swayed sensuously as she worked. His slacks were neither loosely fitted nor overly tight, but he found himself holding his breath as she reached his groin.

And stopped.

Kneeling again, she resumed her work on his other leg, once again halting when she reached his groin. Between her dress, which was sexy enough to be illegal, her snips of the cold scissors and the contrast of her warm fingers on his flesh, he'd grown erect, tightening the material she needed to cut next—making the situation dicey.

Placing her scissors in the scabbard, she unsnapped and unzipped him, then retrieved the scissors and sliced through the waistband with the expertise of a seamstress. In no time at all, his slacks and boxers lay in tatters at his feet.

He thought she might touch him at least a little, but she proceeded to unbutton and cut away his shirt, leaving him bound and naked before her to do with as she pleased. In no hurry, she picked up the scraps of material, bending slowly and sensuously, letting him eye her ultrashort dress, revealing her firm and rounded bottom and the additional fact that she wore no panties. "You going to take off that dress?" he asked, his voice a bit more hoarse than he would have liked.

"Maybe." She removed the belt and scabbard and straightened, a jar in her hands. "Maybe not."

He ignored the jar, kept his gaze on her eyes, which were wide with mystery and passion and a hint of devilry as she surveyed him. Tension made the hair on his neck stand on end. Finally he broke the silence. "So do you like what you see?"

"You could be better."

"Better?"

Her lips turned up in an impish grin. "You aren't sweating, yet."

"That sounds…like a threat."

"A promise." She opened the jar and the scent of mint wafted to him. Dipping her hands into the vanilla-colored cream, she removed a generous amount. "You see I made several interesting discoveries while I was gone."

She was deliberately baiting him, smoothing the cream in her palm, waiting for him to squirm. Well, he was squirming all right—in anticipation.

But tied to the leather pole, he couldn't move. He could only wait for her to come to him.

To give her full credit, she looked magnificent standing there taking full control, not the least bit embarrassed by their love play. And it hit him like a right jab to the jaw—he loved her or he would never trust her so much.

He loved her. Loved her boldness. Loved the brazen look in her eyes. Loved the way she intended to take full advantage of the situation.

He loved her. It was a hell of a time to discover his feelings. He knew it created all kinds of problems, but he put them aside. There were times to live in the moment, and this was one of them.

Her low-cut dress shifted, and he caught the tantalizing sight of a hardened nipple before her movement once again hid her breast from view. The oh-so-short hem teased him with shadows and flashes of a tempting thigh and secret hollows where his fingers itched to delve. Fingers that were restrained above his head.

"What discoveries did you make?" he asked, forcing his gaze to the cream in her hands before that dress drove him crazy with lust. He was already rock hard, aching for her to touch him, and all she'd done was cut off his clothes and appear before him in a scrap of shimmering gold that had all his senses firing on full alert.

He could have sworn he'd caught a whiff of her feminine arousal. Saw a tiny tremor of delight as she boldly eyed him. Heard her draw in a choked breath of appreciation as he stood proudly before her.

She'd taken her time answering him. "This place stocks all kinds of toys."

"You do have a condom, don't you?"

"Oh, we won't be needing that," she whispered, "until later. Much later."

The green flames of heat in her hazel eyes had him testing the strength of the leather wrist guards. He couldn't budge and he didn't know whether to be glad or sad or mad.

If he was free, that dress with so many holes, yet not quite enough of them, would be tossed on the floor. He would have her in his arms, and he would be tasting her flesh—not biting his lip so he wouldn't plead for her touch. Not waiting for a first caress, his stomach tight with tension, his lungs burning to draw in air.

He fought for a semblance of control. "So what…kind of toys interest you?"

"This kind." A heady smile in her eyes, she held out her hands to him palms up, her nails glistening with the cream.

"Care to be more explicit?"

"I prefer to show you." She stepped closer, placed her hands on his hips.

He expected her to grab his straining sex. She didn't.

Instead, she smoothed the cream onto his hips and then onto his buttocks. The cream was cold, and the post at his back angled forward just slightly enough so that she had complete access to his butt.

She took full advantage, not missing one centimeter of flesh, delving into every curve and hollow, taking her time, enjoying the feel of flesh against flesh, driving him crazy for more. The icy sensation disappeared, flushed away by newly forming heat. Everywhere she touched, first ice, then warmth licked his skin, inciting a riot of desire.

The blood in his body seemed drawn to the heat. If he didn't know better, he'd have guessed his straining erection had grown another inch. Skin hot enough to torch a rocket, he craved to plunge inside her and ignite her passion.

He spoke between gritted teeth. "Woman, do you have any idea what you're doing to me?"

"Tell me," she demanded, her hands, now on his nipples, twisting, tweaking, taunting, her delectable mouth inches from him as she knelt on the stool before him, her manner as far from a supplicant's as he was from gaining his freedom.

Heat spiraled through his chest and his lungs caught fire. "Kiss me."

She nipped his lower jaw. "Where?"

He lowered his head to cover her lips and drink from her essence, and she retreated, enough to make him groan with frustration. "My mouth. Kiss my mouth."

"As you wish." She spoke lightly, but her eyes were dark with desire.

While he wished for her to press herself against him, rub her breasts against his chest, she allowed only their lips to touch. His tongue found hers in a maddening taste of desire, and then she escaped, leaving him starving. "That wasn't much of a kiss."

She raised an eyebrow. "Was that a complaint?"

"You know making love is a lot like winning the lottery."

She placed her heated palms on his chest and let them trail down slowly to his waist. "Really?"

"The probability of winning is slightly greater if you buy a ticket."

She chuckled, her fingers dipping below his waist. "I have my ticket. And I'm going to win. I just have to decide when to cash in."

He was going to break into an all-over sweat if she didn't touch him soon. "I might have something to do with when you cash in."

Her hands almost reached the spot he wanted them most. His muscles tightened; he held his breath in anticipation. Then she stepped back. "I have just the thing to keep you in check."

He wondered if it was possible to have an orgasm without one touch. Lord, the cream she'd massaged into his skin had him as jumpy and ready to pop as water on a hot frying pan.

And once again, she'd turned away from him to

rummage through her pack of toys. When she bent over, her dress rose so high on her legs that her blond curls taunted him. Sweat on his brow beaded as he tried to tell himself that the waiting wouldn't kill him.

When she turned around, one perfect, rose-tipped breast clearly visible, he yanked hard on his restraints despite his former vow to be patient. Her partial nudity, the heat of her smile and especially the turned-on look in her eyes had him ready to pounce on her, rip off that see-through dress and take her right now.

Through a haze of desire, he glanced at her hands. Hands that were finally moving in the right direction. His body tightened, gathering for release.

He was so close. Tension gripped him, drawing him into a tense, almost painful knot of need.

Finally her fingers closed around him, but not quite in a caress. Twisting in his bindings, wild with need, he glanced down to see her slipping a circular rubber piece of tubing that looked like a twist tie over his erection. Lightly, ever so lightly, she skimmed the circular tube down to the base of his sex, her fingers teasingly refusing to give him the pressure he needed.

He tugged again on the bonds, his muscles flexing futilely. "What the hell?"

She licked her lips, seemingly fascinated by his throbbing member. "I'm taking control."

And then her head dipped over him, her mouth warm, wet and hot. He couldn't wait to burst, not another second.

The sudden tightening at the base of his shaft prevented his release. She'd constricted the tubing, stopped his orgasm, and he let out a growl of futility.

"Watch me," she commanded. She stood before him and slowly removed the scrap of a dress, letting him feast his gaze on her loveliness. She cupped her breasts, holding herself up to him. "Would *you* like to do this?"

"Yes." His tone was husky, begging.

Her hand brushed the curls between her thighs. "Or perhaps you'd like to touch me here?"

*God, yes.* He slammed his head back into the leather post, his teeth clenched as she came to him, caressed him with her mouth and tongue, working sorcery, whipping him to a tormenting place he'd never been, holding him on the brink between hell and nirvana. His muscles trembled, his knees barely held his weight, and his mind could only think of one thing.

Release.

He had to have her. Now.

But she was making him take more than he'd thought possible. Pushing his body, taunting his mind until he quivered, the strain drawing his body into a bow of need.

He should have expected her to tighten that damn tube again. He'd forgotten what she could do, lost in sensation, until again, she halted his release, tightening the loop, keeping him balanced on a tightwire of need.

"Brittany...you've kept me here long—"

"Enough." She removed the loop from his shaft

and sheathed him in a condom. Kneeling she untied his feet, then stood on the stool to undo his wrists, her hands shaking with impatience, biting her lip.

Finally he was free. She stepped off the stool.

He couldn't wait a second. He tackled her onto the carpet. Plunged into her, fast, furious, frenzied.

Hot. Tight. Wet. She welcomed him home.

"I love you," he growled fiercely in her ear, taking her mouth in his, demanding a kiss that held back nothing.

She gave as good as she got, her hips thrashing, gyrating, matching his thrust for thrust.

"I can't...wait."

"Good."

He exploded, seeing stars, and all the while he gathered her close, unwilling to let go. Not ever.

It took several long minutes to recover, before he could speak. Awe at his experience roughened his tone. "You were—"

"Good?"

"Bad. Very, very bad."

She held him close, her fingers threading through his hair. "Poor baby. I thought you could take a little teasing."

"A little? I thought my thumping heart might blow through my chest."

"How romantic. I guess I shouldn't have tortured you."

"Babe, you can torture me anytime, anywhere."

She snuggled against him. "Is that what it'll take for you to tell me again you love me?"

He kissed her forehead. "You have no idea how much I love you."

She raised herself on her elbow and looked at him. "It wasn't simply a declaration in the heat of passion?"

"It was. I also love you when you're acting like the Ice Princess. Or when you're defending Lyle."

"Damn!"

"What?"

"I got so caught up in playing with you, I forgot I wasn't going to free you until you changed your mind about letting Lyle stay here with my mother."

"Don't worry. I'll square things with the admiral."

"How?"

"Since he lied to me, he'll feel guilty. I'll use that to get him to lay off Lyle." He chuckled. "So passion made you forget your evil plan?"

She looked at him hopefully. "I don't suppose you'll let me tie you up again?"

"I might, but you should probably know that I'd already decided to let Lyle stay before he strung me up for you to toast."

"Why didn't you say so?"

"And give you an excuse to cut me free when I was having so much fun?"

She nipped him.

"Ow."

"You deserve to be bitten."

He adored her teasing him. "Why?"

"You're sneaky and deceptive. You think you

might come up with a way to get yourself tied up again?''

"I might. Under one condition."

"What?"

"You could extend my contract."

"For how long?"

"Indefinitely."

# *Epilogue*

*One year later*

CONSIDERING THE AMOUNT Mrs. Brittany Hunter had paid for her designer lavender wedding gown, she ought to have worn it for a year, but she was more than eager to slip into something more comfortable by the time she and Chad arrived in Eden for their honeymoon.

Ever since the limo pulled through Eden's gates twenty minutes earlier, Brittany's nerves had leaped in expectation. "I asked the driver to drop us off at one of the private rooms I reserved especially for us," she told her new husband sitting beside her on the plush white leather. Although he looked elegant in his navy uniform, she couldn't wait to be alone together as man and wife so she could undress him.

"Which room?" he asked her, his fingers playing with one of the pearl buttons of her bodice.

"It's a surprise."

He raised a commanding eyebrow. "Like asking Judge Laurel Carson to marry us?"

Back from a classified mission, Chad had flown in at the last minute, so all the wedding arrangements had been left up to her. But she'd been involved with feeding the victims of a hurricane in Texas, so Samantha had taken over the wedding planning with her usual aplomb and the ceremony and reception had come off without a hitch.

"Laurel would have been insulted if we'd asked anyone else to officiate. You didn't mind, did you?"

A playful grin turned up one corner of his mouth. "She pinched my butt again. There may be a bruise or two."

"Aurora told me as much. Francois suggested I kiss it and make it all better." She chuckled. "Since he's in medical school now, maybe I'll take his advice."

He swallowed hard, his eyes flaring with interest. "I told Samantha and Lyle not to expect to see us for a few days. I should have told them a few weeks."

"Mother will understand. In fact, with Lyle to keep her company, she may not even notice." Brittany shot Chad a sideways glance. "You think you'll have had enough of me in just a few weeks?"

He pulled her close. "This is Eden, babe." He tipped up her chin, teasing her in a way she'd come to adore. "And in Eden no one ever gets enough."

Her heart fluttered with honeymoon jitters and sensual anticipation at sharing her days and nights with the love of her life. She laid her cheek against his chest, taking pleasure in the fast beat of his heart, the strong arm curving over her shoulder.

She tried to arouse him by allowing a provocative edge to hone her question. "So you don't mind being my adoring love slave, ready to obey my every command?''

He shrugged, his broad shoulders straining his uniform, his voice husky. ''You enslaved me from the moment we met. I'd fight you like hell...if you ever try to let me go.''

''I like that in a husband.''

''What?''

''You know exactly what you want.''

''What I want is you.''

''You're going to want me all right.''

The limo stopped. She shot Chad her most mischievous smile, reached into her purse and pulled out the perfect honeymoon accessories—a pair of handcuffs and a blindfold. ''It's not just your heart I want to enslave, but your body, too.''

He held out his wrists. She snapped on the cuffs and he leaned over to kiss her. ''Babe, I'm all yours.''

### The Cities
New York, Houston, Seattle

### The Singles
Dating dropouts
Chelsea Brockway, Gwen Kempner, Kate Talavera

### The Solution—THE SKIRT!

*Can a skirt really act as a man magnet?* These three
hopeful heroines are dying to find out! But once
they do, how will they know if the men of their
dreams really want *them*…or if the guys are just
making love under the influence?

*Find out in…*

Temptation #860—*MOONSTRUCK IN MANHATTAN*
by Cara Summers, December 2001

Temptation #864—*TEMPTED IN TEXAS*
by Heather MacAllister, January 2002

Temptation #868—*SEDUCED IN SEATTLE*
by Kristin Gabriel, February 2002

**It's a dating
wasteland out there!**

# This Mother's Day
# Give Your Mom
 # A Royal Treat

Win a fabulous one-week vacation in
Puerto Rico for you and your mother at
the luxurious Inter-Continental San Juan
Resort & Casino. The prize includes round
trip airfare for two, breakfast daily and a
mother and daughter day of beauty
at the beachfront hotel's spa.

## INTER·CONTINENTAL
### San Juan
#### RESORT & CASINO

## Here's all you have to do:

Tell us in 100 words or less how your
mother helped with the romance in your
life. It may be a story about your engagement,
wedding or those boyfriends when you were
a teenager or any other romantic advice
from your mother. The entry will be judged
based on its originality, emotionally
compelling nature and sincerity.
See official rules on following page.

**Send your entry to:**
Mother's Day Contest

| **In Canada** | **In U.S.A.** |
|---|---|
| P.O. Box 637 | P.O. Box 9076 |
| Fort Erie, Ontario | 3010 Walden Ave. |
| L2A 5X3 | Buffalo, NY |
| | 14269-9076 |

**Or enter online at www.eHarlequin.com**

All entries must be postmarked by April 1, 2002.
Winner will be announced May 1, 2002. Contest open to
Canadian and U.S. residents who are 18 years of age and older.
No purchase necessary to enter. Void where prohibited.

PRROY